All the
Charli...

DIE HARD
MOD

Charlie McQuaker

Pulp Press

For more information please visit
www.pulppress.co.uk
www.myspace.com/pulppress
or email **answers@pulppress.co.uk**

First published in Great Britain by Pulp Press

All paper used in the printing of this book has been made
from wood grown in managed, sustainable forests.

ISBN13: 978-1-907499-20-3

Printed and bound in the UK
Pulp Press is an imprint of Indepenpress Publishing Limited
25 Eastern Place
Brighton
BN2 1GJ

A catalogue record of this book is available from
the British Library

Cover design by Alex Young
www.brainofalexyoung.com

*For all my dear Brightonian and Belfastard friends,
especially Danny for keepin' da faith and Hannah for
checkin' da words...*

1

Steve Milliken was cruising along the Antrim Coast on his Lambretta with an achingly pretty brunette behind him, her arms wrapped tightly around his waist. He was fairly certain that they would shag each other's brains out when they got to the cosy B & B in Portstewart. Oh, sweet Jeanie. What he wouldn't give to re-live the three months of bliss that he'd shared with her the previous summer. She was a free spirit with a bit of a wild streak and they'd had a blast.

A continuous loud thudding on Steve's front door jolted him back into the reality of a two-up, two-down terrace in rainy North Belfast in late June. 'What the fuck?' he mumbled, pushing his duvet aside with a raging hard-on poking out of his boxer shorts. He quickly made himself decent and stumbled down the stairs past his framed 1965 poster of The Small Faces. It was bound to be his housemate Doug misplacing his keys again after another night on the piss.

When Steve opened the door, he was greeted with a headbutt followed by a boot in the groin. Sprawled out on the floor, he looked up and saw Trevor McCann, UDA battalion leader and local entrepreneur. Trevor was accompanied by Donzo – a gormless-looking 18-stone tattooed skinhead brandishing a baseball bat, which was swiftly aimed at the The Small Faces.

'Stupid lukkin' wee cunts,' muttered Donzo.

Trevor switched on the living room light to give his side-kick a better view of the widescreen TV, hi-fi and Steve's other cherished 1960s Mod memorabilia which was promptly given the same treatment.

Trevor aimed another kick, this time right into Steve's stomach.

'Fuckin' weirdo,' said Trevor

'Jesus, Trevor,' spluttered Steve.

'What's this about?'

Trevor laughed from the depths of his fat gut and then spat straight into Steve's face.

'You fuckin' know rightly what it's about. You know who runs things round here but ye still go and sell dope to them students.'

Steve groped past the pain of the earlier headbutt to remember his journey home from the pub the previous Saturday. He and Doug had stumbled into a party and having shared a few joints with their hosts, they were asked if they wouldn't mind selling some of their large lump of hash. More out of politeness than anything else, Steve had sold them a tenner's worth without giving it much thought.

'Ach Trevor, I'm not tryin' to be a dealer or anythin'… I swear to fuck I'm not… look, could we not just forget it… it won't happen again.'

Trevor had his back turned to Steve and was flicking through his 500-strong collection of vintage 45s. He pulled out *Cry Baby* by John Lee Hooker on the Fortune label. Steve had seen it on Ebay for £200 but loved the record too much to consider selling his copy.

'What the fuck's this shite? John Lee Hooker? What kinda fuckin' name's that? Was his oul' ma a prozzie or somethin'?'

Trevor looked closer at the label and chuckled to himself.

'Cry Baby? Aye, a bit like the fuckin' fruit who owns it.'

With that, he turned round, stared at Steve with a grin and snapped the record in two.

'Byesy, wysesy John Lee Hooker, was a pleasure knowin' ye, whoever the fuck ye are.'

Moist-eyed, Steve dragged himself off the floor and slowly walked towards his tormentor, raising his arms in surrender.

'Listen Trevor… I know I was a dick for sellin' blow to them students. Look, if I just keep out of yer way and swear not to flog any hash to anyone ever again… c'mon mate, giv-vus a break.'

Trevor grabbed Steve by the throat, pulled his face toward his and eye-balled him. Steve could smell booze on his breath and there was a tell-tale deadness in his coked-up eyes

'Don't ever fuckin' call me mate, right? Yer no fuckin' mate 'o mine with yer dopey fuckin' haircut and yer fruity clothes and yer oul' music that no-one's ever heard of… but its not just about sellin' that blow, ye know that, don't ye?'

Steve racked his brains thinking about other possible transgressions. There was the night he was dressed up to the nines in his best Mod gear when he saw Trevor coming towards him in the street. To avoid drawing attention to himself, he'd tried staring into the middle-distance. This had prompted Trevor to say 'who the fuck do ye think you're avoidin' eye-contact with, ye fuckin' fruit?' But he must have been feeling lenient that time because despite the intimidating words, Steve had been able to keep walking, unscathed.

'Alright dip-shit, I'll fuckin' spell it out for ye. Where the fuck's yer fleg for the twelfth?' Steve was staunchly non-sectarian and hated the Orange Order's marching season and their yearly commemoration of a three-hundred-year-old Protestant victory. He just hadn't considered that he'd betray his lack of enthusiasm for the Loyalist cause by not joining his neighbours in displaying Union Jacks or Ulster flags at the front of their homes. 'I, I just haven't got round to sortin' it,' said Steve, his voice quivering. Trevor landed another swift head-butt on him

'Haven't got round to it, yer fuckin' arse. Anyone round here with an ounce of loyalty in their bones gets the oul' flegs out weeks before the twelfth and if they're worth their salt they fuckin' keep 'em out for the rest of the summer. Don't act the innocent with me… you've never bothered yer hole to put out a fleg and ye were so fuckin' stupid that ye thought no-one would notice.'

'I'll get a fleg out straight away, I swear, Trevor… I've got a Northern Ireland football one, will that do?'

'No that fuckin' won't do… I hate them Norn Iron flegs… far to fuckin' Irish-lukkin' with that Celtic cross and the shamrocks 'n all… get a Union Jack sorted, alright?'

Steve nodded.

'Aye Trevor, consider it done.'

Trevor and his goon looked around the room and seemed pleased with their handiwork until Donzo spotted a black

and white photograph of Steve's late parents on the mantel-piece. He picked it up for closer scrutiny. 'Hey look, Trevor, this must be his ma and da… luk at the gear they're wearin'.'
The photo, taken on their honeymoon in 1968, had particular sentimental value for Steve as they both sported the arche-typal 60s clothes and hairstyles that he'd come to love when he became an obsessive Paul Weller fan as a teenager in the 90s.

Trevor grabbed the picture, stared at it and then looked at Steve.

'Yer man here's a friggin' head-the-ball… he wants to luk just like his oul' ma and da did forty fuckin' years ago… the fella's a freak.'

Trevor dropped the picture on the floor and ground his heel into the glass.

'Alright then, I think he's got the message, Donzo. Let's get outta this shite-hole.'

As he followed Donzo out the door, Trevor turned to give Steve a parting shot.

'By the way, fuck-head, we bumped into yer bum-chum Doug earlier. Had a nice wee chat with him too even though we did most of the talkin', if ye catch my drift. Just thought ye should know that ye might not recognise yer mate next time ye see him.'

2

Steve managed to drag his bruised body upstairs to his bedroom and slept fitfully but during his last dream before waking, he was back with Jeanie again. She was kissing his forehead, running her fingers through his hair and whispering sweetly. 'I've missed you too darlin', you'll never know how much... I'm sorry I just disappeared like that without explaining... everything's gonna be alright now, I swear it is.'

Steve woke with a smile but after a few seconds the previous night's events shot back into his consciousness and a sense of dread swamped him. He lay and pondered his predicament. He'd always had his doubts about buying a house in such a rough area but it was the best he could afford on a construction worker's salary and with the recent surge in Belfast's fortunes, he hoped it would one day be more than a no-hope Loyalist ghetto. Five years on he was more realistic about the chances of this ever happening.

While the outside world looked on approvingly at how the peace process was transforming life in the city, Trevor and his fellow paramilitaries had maintained a grip on their patch and were still getting away with their drug-dealing and extortion because nobody would risk their skin bearing witness against them in court.

There wasn't much to keep Steve in Northern Ireland. His parents had died in quick succession when they were still in their early sixties. Heavy smoking and a typical Ulster diet of daily fry-ups, copious red meat and a fair amount of hard liquor hadn't exactly helped them to fend off the Big C. He had an elder brother, Joe, a God-botherer living in Ballymena with his wife and kids, but Joe took a dim view of his kid brother's heathen ways. The last time they'd seen each other was at their mother's funeral three years before.

Since the short-lived but intense relationship with Jeanie, there had been no woman in Steve's life either. And the goodbye note she'd put through his letterbox ('Steve, I'm so sorry if this hurts you but I've got to get away for a while. It's nothing that you've done, I promise. Take care, love, Jeanie') had hardly brought him closure.

As Steve lay there feeling sorry for himself, he was thinking that it was alright for his flatmate. After his beating from Trevor and Donzo, Doug would at least have been able to crawl round to his girlfriend Suzie's flat which was only a few streets away. She was a nurse and would be able to attend to his wounds and give him some TLC. Steve pictured Doug recuperating in bed while Suzie brought him a nice big Ulster fry and a mug of tea.

Steve was dreading having to survey the previous night's damage but knew he'd have to eventually. He got up and looked at his reflection in the bedroom mirror. He was relieved that what Jeanie had once jokingly called his 'ageing pretty boy kind of good looks' remained unspoilt and he was able to rearrange his thick fringe to cover the huge throbbing bruise on his forehead.

Next to the mirror, Steve had a framed print of George Best from 1967 to which he attached almost religious significance. Best, with the ball at his feet and a haircut not dissimilar to Steve's own, imperiously beckoned to a brutish opponent to try to take the ball off him. Looking at the picture always gave Steve a lift. He reckoned it got to the core of what it meant to be a Belfast boy. A stubborn, contrary, defiant brand of underdog individualism. 'Don't let the bastards grind ye down, eh Geordie?' said Steve as he left the bedroom. 'Fuck the lot of 'em.'

Downstairs, the place was a mess. Flinching at the memory of the violence Trevor and his henchman had handed out, Steve fetched a dust pan and brush and set about clearing up the broken glass. After some hoovering and tidying-up, the place looked a lot better but his TV and stereo were unsalvageable. He brought a portable CD player down from his bedroom, got a beer from the fridge and put on *Otis Blue* by Otis Redding. 'Otis knew a bit about suffering' thought Steve as he curled up on his sofa in the foetal position.

The last track on the album came on and it made Steve think about Jeanie again. '*You don't miss your water 'til your well runs dry*… aye, yer fuckin' right there, Otis' he thought. As the song faded, Steve could feel his belly rumbling and he got up in search of some comfort food. He made himself a curry-flavoured Pot Noodle and a couple of slices of thick white toast dripping with butter.

With his hunger satisfied, he felt in the mood for some comfort viewing too. The movie that did it for him every time was *Quadrophenia* which he'd been obsessed with since he first saw it as a fifteen year-old. No matter how many times he watched it, he felt the same vicarious thrill as the cavalcade of scooters sped down to Brighton for the Mods' Bank Holiday adventures. And as for his hero Jimmy's knee-trembler down a back alley with the gorgeous Stef, it was still one of his favourite masturbation fantasies. 'One for the wank jukebox, eh Steve?' Doug always said. Steve stared mournfully at the hole in the middle of his telly before discovering that his DVD player worked perfectly well once he connected it to the portable he usually kept in the kitchen. 'Up yours, Trevor' whispered Steve as he settled down.

The movie had reached the dire moment when a postman drives over Jimmy's beloved scooter which is when a grim possibility occurred to Steve. 'Oh fuck... what about my Lambretta?' He got off the sofa and went to open his front door to check the parking space outside. His battered scooter was lying on its side and Trevor and Donzo had ensured that it was a write-off. Steve stood gawping helplessly at the wreckage while his phone began ringing indoors. He shuffled back inside and answered it with a forlorn-sounding 'hello'.

'Jesus Steve, ye need to sort out yer phone manner there, luv... what's up?' It was Doug's girlfriend. 'Don't even ask, Suze... let's just say that I'll be glad when today's over... anyway, nice to hear a friendly voice, how can I help ye?'

'Just lookin' for that no-good boyfriend of mine... I suppose he's comatose on the sofa after another night on the lash? The useless git was meant to grab a pizza and come round mine after he'd been to the pub but he was a no-show and his mobile keeps goin' to voicemail... he'd better have a good apology ready… could ye put him on?… Steve? Are ye still there? Don't you be coverin' for him, Steve… c'mon, what's happened this time?'

Steve had a fair idea what might have happened. He slowly put the phone down and projectile vomited chunks of Pot Noodle and toast all over his newly-vacuumed carpet.

3

Later that evening, the UTV news team provided Steve and Suzie with details of Doug's whereabouts.

'The body of local man Douglas McConville, aged 32, has been found in Fortwilliam Park, North Belfast. Police are treating the death as suspicious and are appealing for witnesses, or anyone who may be able to assist them with their inquiries into the events that led to Mr. McConville's death, to come forward. The deceased is described as having cropped blonde hair and was wearing a white Fred Perry polo shirt, jeans and desert boots.'

Steve went round to Suzie's flat and comforted her as she wept. She was a slight, petite and boyish-looking red-head and felt as delicate as a child as he stood with his arms around her. It reminded him of hugging his skinny, ten-year old nephew after his mother's funeral. Steve's own tears hadn't started to flow yet and he trembled with the effort of holding them back. Suzie had a bottle of Bushmills in her kitchen and he'd poured them each a treble measure. When they sat down on her sofa, he downed his in one but hers remained untouched.

'Why would anyone want to hurt Doug?' she pleaded.

'Thing is luv, I had some visitors last night …'

When Steve told Suzie about Trevor and Donzo, her fists started flailing.

'You and your fuckin' dope-smokin'… Doug was never into that shit until he started living with you and none of this would have happened if…'

Steve grabbed her wrists and shouted back at her.

'For fuck's sake Suzie, don't start taking it out on me. My best mate's dead and my cards marked now too. I reckon them psychos were so coked-up they didn't realise they'd killed Doug and now they'll be after me to make sure I keep my mouth shut. It's probably not a good idea for me to be here 'cos the word might get around and they'll suss that I've blabbed to you.'

Steve hugged Suzie and tried to wipe her tears away.

'Look luv… the peelers have been wantin' to pin something on Trevor for years and they're bound to have his DNA on file. If their forensic team are any fuckin' use at all, they'll be able to get the evidence they need. It's best if I get outta town and lay low for a while, you understand?'

Suzie nodded.

'Get yerself over to yer ma's, Suzie… a girl needs her ma at a time like this, eh?'

Steve gave Suzie a parting hug and got out of her flat, fast.

4

When Steve got to the end of his street, he checked to see if anyone he needed to avoid was hanging around his house but it just felt like a typical Sunday night. The Maguires' Jack Russell was barking his head off at nothing in particular and he could see the old couple from Number 38 on their way to the evening service while Sammy Armstrong, his alcoholic next door neighbour, staggered home from the off-licence with a few cans of Tennents Super. Steve sauntered up to his front door, had one last glance around the street and let himself in. He went up to his bedroom, threw some clothes and toiletries into a hold-all, switched all the lights off and split.

On the Shore Road, Steve hopped onto a bus to take him into the city centre. Aside from the type of quizzical looks his Mod appearance usually attracted, no-one on the bus seemed to notice how jittery he was. His heart was racing but anxiety helped focus his mind. He had to get out of Belfast but where was he going to go? He had a cousin he was close to in Edinburgh but he was married with three kids one of whom was severely disabled so he couldn't imagine he'd be welcomed with open arms there. There was his mate Tim who'd immigrated to Toronto but the air fare would wipe out half his savings. But at least tonight he'd be able to stay with Johnny Bell, one of his Mod associates who put on a low-key 60s night upstairs at The Garrick Bar on the last Sunday of every month. Johnny had a decent-sized flat in the bohemian area around Queen's University in the south side of the city. Nice and civilised and not the sort of place that he'd be likely to bump into Trevor and Donzo.

Steve got off the bus at the City Hall and when he arrived at The Garrick, there were about a dozen of the usual suspects trying to out-do each other in 60s retro style. Wee Davy looked pretty sharp in his blue three-button mohair suit set off with a paisley scarf and a French crop haircut. There were a couple of heavily-made-up girls with Mary Quant hairstyles and skimpy psychedelic-patterned dresses but they were a little too podgy to carry the look off with much success.

Johnny was behind the decks playing Georgie Fame's *Somebody Stole My Thunder* and with the kind of lean frame that best suits Mod fashion, he looked the coolest of the bunch with a dark green cashmere polo-neck and a haircut modelled on Jeff Beck in 1968. He beckoned Steve to come over and join him and hugged him as the tune blasted out and a smattering of Mods shuffled nonchalantly around the dance-floor.

'Jesus Steve, how are ye hombre?' said Johnny. 'I heard all about Doug. The whole crew are really shook up about it. Ye missed a wee announcement I made earlier. I know it might not mean much but I just dedicated tonight to him. The girls have been bawling their eyes out, so they have.'

The tender concern in Johnny's eyes made Steve feel like crying himself but he needed to keep it together.

'I'm all the better for seein' you mate… can't face being in the house alone tonight so hope its okay if I crash at yours.'

Johnny hugged him again.

'Nae bother amigo… it's the least I can do.'

Steve let Johnny get on with his DJ duties and spent the rest of the night in a corner at the back, cradling his Guinness as each of the Mods took turns to come over and offer their condolences. The place filled out with students and random drinkers and as the dancing intensified to the sound of The Spencer Davis Group's *I'm a Man*, Steve felt numb to the hubbub around him. Wee Davy was the last to come over and talk to him. He was always buzzing on some substance or another but his heart was in the right place.

'Stevie boy, I know you've heard it all tonight mate but I just wanted to tell ya that I thought Doug was a top man. See when I was skint, the fella would always stand me drinks all night… and he was great crack, so he was. I know he was yer best mucker 'n all, must be hard to get yer head around… how are ye bearin' up, kid?'

Steve patted Davy's shoulder affectionately.

'It's kind of you to ask Davy and I'm not bein' funny but I'm really tired of talkin' about how I'm feelin'. C'mon mate, tell us how you've been. What have ye been up to lately?'

'Ach just the same stuff, Steve. Still workin' in that shop in the arcade that sells the second-hand retro gear. Best crack I've had lately was the other weekend. Me and my girl went over for a Mod bash in Brighton. I tell ye what, its fuckin' cracker over there, so it is. It's a bit like how you imagine the

60s… folk bein' dead cool 'n friendly 'n all. But you'll never guess what, mate. I was at this wee basement place near the seafront and I coulda sworn I saw that wee girl you went out with, Jeanie. The one that did a disappearin' act on ye, yeah? I said hello when she walked past but she just blanked me. But I swear, Steve, I would bet my whole fuckin' record collection that it was her.'

And with that, Steve knew his escape destination.

5

Steve only managed to get a few hours sleep on Johnny's sofa and at around eight, he could hear his host putting on the kettle in the kitchen.

'Can I have brew, Johnny boy?' he shouted. 'White, one sugar.'

'Was makin' ye one anyway,' replied Johnny. 'Got a wee fry on the go too.'

'Happy days!' said Steve, before the irony of the statement sunk in.

He went through to sit at Johnny's kitchen table and a plate of bacon, egg, sausage, mushrooms, potato bread and soda bread was put in front of him accompanied by a steaming mug of tea. It looked wonderful and it was some comfort to Steve that his appetite hadn't been affected by his woes. 'Boy ye could represent Ulster in the eatin' Olympics, son', his ma used to say.

'So, what's the plan, Steve? Takin' the day off work? I'm sure they'd understand if ye do. Ye gotta do what's best for you at a time like this… be gentle with yerself n' all.'

Johnny's kind sincerity acted like a truth drug on Steve.

'Thing is, mate, I gotta get the fuck outta Belfast.'

'Ye what?'

Steve gave Johnny the low-down on Trevor and Donzo and the Brighton escape plan, hoping that his friend's common sense might provide a clear eye on his predicament.

'Fuckin' hell Steve, if it was anyone but Trevor McCann I'd go straight to the peelers but I can see where yer comin' from… there's a good reason why that fat psycho bastard is still roamin' free. Fuck, remember yer man who started slabberin' to the papers about Trevor sellin' smack to his son…. I saw that poor fucker in his wheelchair around Corn Market the other day…'

'Aye Johnny, and he's upped the ante from knee-cappings and sellin' class As with this particular felony, wouldn't ye say?'

Steve mopped up some egg yolk with the last bit of potato bread and wolfed it down while Johnny poured him another cup of tea.

'So Johnny, I've got if figured out. I'll go to the doc's this mornin' and get signed off work for a couple of months and that'll buy me a bit o' time. He put me on Prozac when I got maself into a state about Jeanie fuckin' off on me so he's already got me down as a sensitive wee soul. I can clear out my savings – that'll give me twelve hundred quid cash to keep me goin'. Once I've done that, I'll be on the flight to Gatwick and then it's straight to sunny Brighton for Stevie boy.'

'What about the peelers, Steve? Have they not talked to you yet? Will they not start thinkin' there's somethin' fishy goin' on if ye just disappear like this?'

'Listen mate, if I start worryin' about the peelers it'll do my head in but I'm not gonna be stupid about it either. I won't be usin' my cash card any more so beyond maybe sussin' out that I've flown to Gatwick, they won't be able to trace where I am and I'll just get maself a new mobile when I hit Brighton.'

'Aye Steve but if they want to, they'll make it their business to catch up with you eventually.'

Steve finished his tea and started fiddling with his chunky silver identity bracelet.

'Look Johnny, if they ever get houl' o'me, I reckon I'll be able to deal with it… I haven't fuckin' done anythin' so what's the worst they can do? I'll just say I needed to get away to get my head showered or somethin'. But if Trevor ever gets houl' o' me, that's a whole different ball game.'

Johnny lifted the empty plates and put them in the sink.

'Guess ye gotta go with yer instinct Steve but why Brighton? I know ye love Quadrophenia 'n all but is that a good enough reason?'

'As good a reason as any, mate… not to mention the fact that Wee Davy swore blind that he saw Jeanie when he was over there on a weekender a wee while back.'

'Listen, Steve. I think you've got enough on your plate without bringin' Jeanie into the equation. I mean, Wee Davy says more than his prayers. He's so off his nut half the time that he was probably hallucinatin'… sees some cute girl with bobbed hair and jumps to the conclusion that it's Jeanie… fella's a fuckin' wingnut.'

'He sounded pretty convinced to me.'

'That's as may be, Steve and I never wanted to say anythin' before 'cos I knew you were cracked-up on her but I'll tell ye now… I know she was gorgeous 'n all but there was just a vibe I got off her that creeped me out… I always thought that girl was bad news… *really* bad news.'

6

Steve arrived at George Best Belfast City Airport with an hour
to spare before his 5.40pm flight. A screen played clips of
Best in his heyday on a continuous loop. 'So what would you
do if you were in my shoes, Geordie?' wondered Steve. 'I
know. You'd start workin' yer charm on the first sexy blonde
you met and offer to share some vino with her on the flight.
She'd fall for your little-boy-lost routine and want to look
after you… she might even be loaded and let ye take refuge
in her penthouse flat… champagne breakfasts every mornin'
and sex on tap…save ye all the bother of tryin' to make yer
way in some strange town...'

In the check-in queue, he clocked a foxy, posh-looking
30-something blonde in a pencil skirt which made the most
of her nicely-shaped backside. Their eyes briefly met and he
smiled at her but she shot him back a look that said 'don't
even think about it, loser.'

'Brighton it is, then,' decided Steve.

After an uneventful flight during which he was stuck between two chubby business men comparing the nightly rates

of upmarket hotels they'd stayed in, Steve arrived at London Gatwick.

The Gatwick to Brighton train was mainly filled with weary, defeated-looking commuters but in the seat facing him were a couple of lads he took to be students. One had opted for the dishevelled, floppy-haired indie look while the other had shoulder-length dreadlocks, a lip-ring and a Free Tibet t-shirt. The indie-looking kid looked impressed by Steve's style.

'Excuse me, mate. Just wondering where you got those boots from. They really look the business.'

Steve had a shiny pair of black Chelsea boots that went well with his check-toothed hipster trousers. He smiled at the compliment.

'Got 'em off Ebay, mate... only a tenner. So what's the crack with you lads? On yer way to Brighton then?'

'Yeah,' said the dreadlocked one. 'Had a bit of a mental one partying in London with mates and just getting back to reality now... we should probably start looking for a summer job now that term's over.'

'So you're Irish, yeah?' asked the indie kid.

'Aye, that's right'

'Cool!'

Steve liked that. He hadn't even had to do anything and he was already deemed 'cool' just by virtue of being Irish. For the rest of the journey, the students were hanging on Steve's every word, with any minor witticism that he delivered in his thick Ulster brogue being greeted with howls of laughter. It looked like Brighton was going to be a doddle.

7

Steve arrived in Brighton with two basic tips from the students ringing in his ears. 'Avoid West Street, mate, especially at weekends… it's full of lairy dickheads. And see the pubs right next to the station? Don't bother, they're crap. Just go down Trafalgar Street and head to the Albert … it's only a minute's walk away'.

The second piece of advice immediately seemed very sound to Steve. There, immortalised in a mural on the side of the pub was his hero, George Best. 'This is my destiny calling,' he thought.

For a Monday night, the place was pretty busy, filled with a ragged, genial-looking assortment of art students, old rockers and booze-hounds. While the juke-box played the opening riff of *Tin Soldier,* his favourite Small Faces tune, Steve felt a life-affirming buzz, sat himself down on a bar stool and tried to get the attention of the tattooed, peroxide blonde barmaid. Next to him, there was a skinny, hollow-cheeked dude with an unruly mop of collar-length brown hair who wouldn't have looked out of place at a psychedelic rave-up in 1967. He was intently mouthing the lyrics of the tune while nursing an empty glass. So could this really be Brighton; the carefree land of kindred spirits that Steve always dreamt it might be? He caught the barmaid's eye.

'Pint of Guinness please luv and whatever this fella here's havin'.'

The recipient of his generosity turned and smiled at him. He looked like he'd had a few but was still keeping it together.

'Cheers boss… don't I know you? We do a gig together one night or something?'

'Nah mate, it's just that anyone who appreciates Tin Soldier is alright by me. I'm Steve by the way… pleased to meet ye.' Steve shook his hand.

'Likewise, boss. I'm Bobby. You're a Belfast Boy yeah? Would know that accent anywhere. So, don't tell me… George Best was the Messiah and Gloria by Them blows the fuck out of anything by English ponces like The Beatles or The Stones …'

'Spot on, Bobby. You're a smart lad.'

'… and let's not forget that the sweat of Belfast ship-yard workers built the mighty Titanic and that your lot were the unsung pioneers of the 17th century who crossed the Atlantic, made Tennessee their own, formed the back-bone of the American revolutionary army and invented country music…'

'Not too keen on the oul' country music so let's leave that bit out,' laughed Steve. 'How the fuck do ye know that stuff?'

'My old man was from Belfast, boss… grew up on all the myths and legends.'

'He sounds like a wise and enlightened fella... here's to yer da, cheers!'

Steve clinked glasses with his new companion and drained his glass. All the stuff he'd heard about English Guinness tasting inferior proved untrue and the agreeable atmosphere in the pub put him in a drinking mood.

'Two more pints please, luv.'

From his stool, Steve could see through to another seated area behind the bar and his heart raced as he saw the slender back of a girl with a sleek black bob and striped t-shirt. He was about to blurt out something but when the girl turned around, although she was quite a looker of similar height and build, she wasn't Jeanie.

Bobby noticed Steve's sudden change in demeanour.

'You alright boss? Look like you've seen a ghost.'

'Yeah, something like that... more a case of mistaken identity.'

Bobby looked bemused but didn't pursue the matter any further.

'So what brings you to Brighton?'

Steve gestured to their surroundings.

'I wanted a bit o' this, mate. I've always heard that Brighton's a tolerant place... I know the tourists are flocking to Belfast 'n all but this is more my kinda town... sort o' place where ye might bump into folk who know the lyrics to Tin Soldier and where ye don't get any hassle if ye choose to dress differently to every other spidey wanker.'

'Spidey? Whaddya mean, boss?'

'Sorry mate... I think ye say chavvy over here, don't ye?'

'Well I grew up in a dodgy estate in Hackney so I can't say I'm in a position to look down on the rougher elements but the clobber that you see some of the youth wearing these days, it's diabolical… 'orrible white trainers, tracksuit bottoms, hoodies and baseball caps… shocking.'

'Too fuckin' right… just 'cos ye grow up poor, shouldn't mean that ye don't have any class.'

The pair clinked glasses again and continued chatting. Bobby told Steve how he made a few quid as a musician doing pub gigs with a soul covers band but when that kind of employment was thin on the ground, he'd turn his hand to anything… labouring, painting and decorating… whatever it took to get by. Steve decided to keep schtum about his real reasons for coming to Brighton. It would make life simpler if he just said that he fancied being in a happening seaside town for the summer. After getting another round of pints in, Bobby gave Steve a mischievous look.

'Hey boss,' he whispered. 'If you fancy making a night of it, you could have a dab of this and we could go to this club I know… a lot of the art school chicks go there… they play a lot of trendy indie shit but the totty makes up for it.'

Bobby quickly opened his palm and showed Steve an open bag of white crystallised powder.

'MDMA yeah?'

'The very thing… its quite pokey though, so go easy.'

Steve had a glance around to make sure that he was being discreet, licked his right index finger, dipped it into the bag and then quickly put the substance in his mouth.

Towards the end of his pint, Steve felt the drug kick in as The Byrds's *Mr, Tambourine Man* blasted out of the jukebox.

The colour of his companion's shirt now seemed the bluest of any blue Steve could imagine and the euphoric chemical rush seemed to obliterate all the dreadful events of the weekend. The music, which Steve loved anyway, suddenly seemed even more magical and profound.

'Fuckin' hell Bobby, I'm flyin'.'

'You said it, boss... so let's get outta here and fly on down to The Joint to check out the talent.'

8

If Steve had thought the Albert was agreeable, he found The Joint even more so. Having checked in his holdall at the cloakroom, he followed Bobby down a spiral staircase into a dimly-lit basement decorated with kitsch, vaguely erotic murals. The venue was rammed with good-looking scenesters making shapes to a tune Steve quite liked called *Jerk it Out* by The Caesars. Steve reckoned it wasn't a patch on the original 60s stuff but it was a pretty decent pastiche. It certainly provided a worthy excuse for joining in with the dancing.

Steve felt such a big emotional connection with music that he was an effortlessly graceful dancer. While a lot of his Mod friends in Belfast would stiffly and self-consciously try to ape dance moves that they'd seen in old episodes of *Ready Steady Go* from the 60s, Steve just let his body respond to the groove of the tune and would almost glide around the dance floor, with a beatific smile on his face.

In true Mod spirit, however, he was a terrible snob and if a tune offended his taste, he'd stop dancing and hang around the bar until it was over. As Bobby was getting more beers in, Steve couldn't help himself from looking around intently in the hope that Jeanie might be amongst the crowd but after clocking at least three girls with a similar black bob, he realised that he needed to stop his chemically-enhanced imagination running away with itself.

After three or four mediocre tunes that all reminded him of Joy Division, *Molly's Chambers* by Kings of Leon came on. Bobby was still waiting to get served at the bar but Steve felt like mingling with the revellers, especially as the tune had exactly the type of rhythm that he liked dancing to.

Steve was adept at feigning a lack of interest in what was going on around him on the dance floor but he felt a tantalising sense that a fair-haired girl in a red 'Vintage Vinyl Saved My Soul' t-shirt seemed to be making an effort to dance closer to him. She had a sweet, apple-cheeked face and Steve thought that she looked quite like an *Eastenders* actress from the 90s that he used to fancy. His instincts proved right and soon the girl was dancing right in front of him and looking right into his eyes. She lent closer.

'Didn't think you Mod dudes liked this sort of thing.'

Steve gently put his hand on her neck as he spoke into her ear.

'Sometimes a fella just wants to shake his ass around a dance floor and ye can't always be fussy about what yer shakin' it to.'

The girl giggled flirtatiously.

'Sounds like you put your ass about a little too indiscriminately… I'd watch that.'

Steve laughed.

'Yeah, I might catch indie wanker disease if I'm not careful.'

She scowled in mock indignation.

'I'll have you know that some of my best friends are indie wankers.'

The Kings of Leon tune started cross-fading into *Apply Some Pressure* by Maximo Park and Steve grimaced.

'Talking of indie wankers, I aint dancin' to this shite… fancy a drink? Sorry, I didn't catch yer name?'

'I'm Sally but everyone just calls me Sal. And yours?'

'I'm Steve. It's nice to meet ye Sal. C'mon, let's get away from this dross. It's offensive.'

Sal pulled a face and gave the music a thumbs-down sign in solidarity.

As they walked towards the bar, Steve saw that Bobby was engrossed in conversation with a wasted-looking guy with an impressive afro who had appropriated the bottle of Becks that was intended for him.

The throng at the bar had thinned and Steve quickly got another Becks and a rum and coke for Sal. They managed to secure a couple of seats at a candle-lit alcove at the rear of the club.

Steve now felt pleasantly drunk but still quite lucid as the effects of the MDMA wore off. Sitting next to Sal, he could see that although she wasn't his usual sultry brunette type, she was an attractive girl and her open, smiley manner made him feel relaxed and upbeat.

'I'm guessing you're from Northern Ireland… you sound just like Colin Murray off the radio or that ginger comedian bloke, whatshisname…' said Sal.

'Patrick Kielty' said Steve, cringing. 'Nice to be mentioned in the same breath as those A-listers. Anyway, I'm not really a showbiz fella, more a practical type so if ye know of any jobs goin', I need to fund the rest of this wee seaside break.'

'I'm a teacher so I don't know how much use I'd be with your job-hunting' said Sal. '… but I could ask around.'

'Ach I'm sure I'll have nae bother findin' somethin'. So anyway, who are ye down here with?'

'Oh, just tagging along with a mate and her boyfriend… think they took pity on me or something… knew I needed to get out instead of just lying around watching my West Wing box-sets.'

Sal explained how she'd split up with a long-term partner five months previously and was just tentatively venturing back into the singles world.

'Thing is, I'm pretty self-contained and I'm busy at work during the week but weekends can actually be the hardest… reading the Sunday papers on your own with just Radio 4 for company can really bring on the self-pity sometimes, you know.'

'You're breakin' my heart here, Sal,' said Steve with a grin. 'C'mon, you're not gonna be single for long… you're lovely… ye know you've got really kind eyes, don't ye?'

'Thanks,' she said coyly. 'Windows to the soul and all that. Either means I'm kind-hearted or just too bloody soft, eh?'

Steve looked at her gentle blue eyes intently and concluded that unless his gut instinct was badly betraying him, this girl didn't have a bad bone in her body. He brushed a lock of hair behind her ear and kissed her. Her soft lips eagerly met his and he felt a thrill more real than anything the drugs had offered him earlier.

After their kiss, Steve put his arm around Sal and they held hands as they exchanged stories about their respective lives in Belfast and Brighton. It was getting close to 2 am and lights started to go up. As the other clubbers began filtering out, Steve could see Bobby sat by the bar on his own, supping the remnants of his beer.

'Hey Sal, guess I'd better have a word with the fella I came down here with.' He nodded towards where his new friend was sitting.

'So you're a mate of Bobby's then? That's Brighton for you… never mind six degrees of separation, it's usually just one. My ex, Rich, used to play bass in Bobby's band. Bit of a local character is our Bobby boy. Overdoes the partying a bit too much, bless him, but he's got a heart of gold.'

'Well I'm glad you approve of the company I keep, Sal, 'cos it would be nice to see you again.'

'I'd like that too, Steve. Bobby has my number if you want to get in touch.'

They briefly kissed again before Sal got up to join her friends who were waiting for her at the foot of the stairs. Before leaving, she waved over to Steve again and blew him a parting kiss.

9

Emerging from the club to the sound of seagulls and drunken laughter, Steve and Bobby agreed that they were both feeling peckish. They walked across the road to a fast food place where they each ordered a burger and a can of Coke. They got a window seat and watched random characters in various states of intoxication stumble along West Street.

'Have been meaning to ask ye somethin' Bobby,' said Steve.

'Fire away, boss.'

'Thing is, I haven't sorted maself out with anywhere to stay and was wonderin' if I could crash on yer sofa tonight. There's a youth hostel in Brighton aint there? Was thinkin' of checkin' in there tomorrow.'

'Well you're in luck, boss. My flatmate's staying in New York with his girlfriend and won't be back until the end of August. I could do with the extra cash so if you reckon you could manage fifty quid a week, you can have his room for a while as long as you leave it like you found it.'

Steve shook Bobby's hand.

'It's a deal, mate. Yer a lifesaver, so ye are. I'm pretty well house-trained actually. Ye know the Mod motto, 'clean living under difficult circumstances'? Well that's me to a T, so it is.'

'Well that's handy, boss, 'cos I'm a bit of slob myself,' laughed Bobby. 'C'mon, let's make a move. I'm meant to be on site tomorrow at eight. Got a bit of labouring work at this big Regency gaff that needs gutting.'

'Jesus, yer gonna feel like shit havin' to do some hard graft after a night on the tear,' said Steve, shaking his head.

'I can handle it… get to the caff for about quarter-past seven, couple of bacon sarnies and some strong coffee with three sugars and I'll be right as rain.'

The streets were nearly deserted as they walked along Western Road towards Bobby's flat on Lansdowne Place. At the junction with Montpelier Road, a homeless guy was lying at the corner outside Waitrose supermarket and Steve reached into his pocket to chuck him a few quid. As he did so, a couple of crop-haired geezers in over-sized trainers and tracksuit bottoms appeared from round the corner. One was thick-set and swarthy and wearing a Liverpool top; the other was pale, lanky and rat-faced with an Abercrombie & Fitch t-shirt. They walked straight up to Steve and Bobby.

'Alright lads, 'ows it goin'?' said the stockier of the two, blocking Steve's way on the pavement.

'I'm fuckin' doin' rightly mate but would ye mind gettin' outta my way?'

Bobby chipped in.

'C'mon lads, we're just on our way home… we don't want any hassle.'

The guy refused to budge.

'Just hand over your fuckin' cash you cunts and we'll be done with ya.'

Steve stood his ground and screamed in their faces.

'Look, you arseholes… yer not dealin' with some student poofs here… I'm from fuckin' Belfast so don't try 'n pull yer hard man bullshit with me… get the fuck outta my way or I'll knock yer fuckin' ballix in!'

With that, the rat-faced one produced a blade from his pocket and shoved it against Steve's throat.

'Listen, you cunt… I don't give a fuck if you're from downtown Bronx… givvus your fuckin' wallet, now!'

Steve stood rigid with his arms dangling at his sides as his assailant rummaged in his pockets.

'What have we got here then?'

He opened Steve's wallet and grabbed a bunch of notes out of it.

'Fuckin' 'ell… he's got some 'undred quid notes here and a few fifties… '

No sooner had he grabbed the cash than the muggers were sprinting eastwards down Western Road, leaving Steve and Bobby standing there, stunned.

'Fuckin' 'ell, boss… don't tell me that's the sum total of your cash.'

Steve crouched down to pick up the discarded wallet from the pavement and looked up at Bobby as he checked its contents.

'Well mate… lets just say that I'm well and truly fucked.'

10

When Steve awoke in Bobby's flat at around ten, he was on his own and a night of fearful dreams had left him feeling disorientated and anxious. He went into the kitchen to make himself a cup of tea and found a set of keys, a map of Brighton and a note.

Chin up Belfast Boy. I'll ask the guv'nor at work if he could do with an extra pair of hands so we can sort out your cash-flow problems. Not much grub in the house but you can get a good fry-up in Belchers. I've marked it on the map. Also marked the North Laine area which is coolest place to go for a stroll in this town. How fuckin' good a host am I, eh? Should be back about six. P.S. Flat could do with a bit of a clean if you want to help earn your keep!

The note cheered Steve up and he realised that being befriended by Bobby was one plus that he could draw from the last few days. He made his tea and wandered around the flat as he supped it. Bobby wasn't kidding about it needing a clean. There were ashtrays full of old roaches, empty beer cans and Sunday papers still strewn across the living room floor.

The room was dominated by a 1968 poster of The Beatles that Steve recognised as a still from the promotional film for *Revolution*. Behind the TV there were shelves crammed full of rock 'n roll biographies and DVDs of comedy classics like *This is Spinal Tap* and *Monty Python and the Holy* Grail plus assorted football anthologies. A proper lad's 'back to mine after the pub' kind of flat, he concluded

Steve set about tidying the place up. Once he had, and with the blinds pulled up and sunlight streaming through the Victorian sash windows, it revealed itself to be quite an attractive flat with stripped wooden floors and original cornicing on the high ceilings. If Brighton was the kind of town that someone like Bobby could afford to live in a place like this, it couldn't be all bad.

Steve made himself another cup of tea and flicked through Bobby's CDs. He pulled out *Five Leaves Left* by Nick Drake.

The plaintive melancholy of the album seemed perfect for Steve's mood and halfway through the song *River Man*, he began weeping. Despite everything that had happened to him since Friday night, all the turmoil had remained bottled-up so the outpouring came as a welcome release. Steve knew the tears weren't just for Doug and he felt slightly ashamed when he realised that some of them were shed over a fistful of notes that a pair of scumbags were now probably spending on charlie or smack.

After cleaning up the flat and washing a sink-full of dirty dishes, Steve headed into town with Bobby's map folded in his back pocket. He didn't really fancy a fry-up so he sussed out a route so he could head straight to North Laine via

Western Road and North Street. He was hoping that he might spot some locations from *Quadrophenia* along the way but nothing he saw sparked any recognition.

By the time he reached Gardner Street, Steve had realised that the type of people who would attract curiosity in Belfast because of their quirky appearance seemed to be the norm in Brighton. He'd never seen so many tattoos, piercings and outlandish fashion statements on display in such a concentrated area. On one hand he was impressed by the 'anything goes' atmosphere but at the same time his Northern Irish contrariness made him feel that it was a little too easy to be an individual in Brighton. By its very nature, true rebelliousness needs something to kick against and what would provide a rebel with grist to the mill in a place like this, he wondered?

Walking along Kensington Gardens in the sunshine, his brain went into the default mode of hoping he would spot Jeanie and, just like in the nightclub the previous evening, there was no shortage of look-alikes who'd momentarily set his pulse racing until he realised that it was yet another cutie with a dark bob and a slim physique.

'Snap out of it!' said a voice in his head. 'Listen to yer higher self, ye twat... this Jeanie thing is just piling on the misery... Johnny was right, you've got enough on yer plate already... c'mon, think positive... yer miles from where Trevor and Donzo might find ye, in a place where no-one gives a fuck what ye look like or what religion ye are... Britain's San Francisco... that's what they said in that travel supplement, remember? Down by the seaside... yeah, the sea... that's what ye need!'

On Sydney Street, Steve stopped the first friendly face he saw – a hippy woman with a raggle-taggle pair of kids trailing behind her.

'Sorry to bother ye luv, was just wonderin' what's the easiest way to get to the seafront from here?'

The hippy woman smiled. 'Oh I love that accent… Irish, yeah? Well it's dead easy… just turn round and keep walking in the opposite direction and you'll be there in about ten or fifteen minutes.'

She looked at Steve intently for a few moments.

'Are you okay, man?… I'm just getting an energy off you like something's troubling you? You've been through some bad shit, aint ya?'

Steve was taken aback but touched.

'Well that's true… been through a bit of a rough patch, right enough.'

She lightly stroked the side of his face.

'Maybe meditation would help you… find somewhere quiet and repeat a mantra… you could try 'Om ma ni pad me hum'.'

'… or as they say back home, I could just take a big wise-up tablet.'

The hippy woman looked confused.

'Well whatever works for you, man. Just take it easy, yeah?'

One of the kids was tugging on her flowing Indian dress and she smiled again at Steve before walking towards The Dumb Waiter café where a guy with dreadlocks was sat at the window beckoning her to join him.

Steve followed her directions and soon he was on Ship Street where the sea became visible for the first time. He crossed Kings Road and went to lean on the railings so he could survey the coastline properly. Looking east, Steve experienced a child-like thrill to see the tacky splendour of the Palace Pier and felt magnetically drawn towards it, not least because he was getting hungry and knew that it would be somewhere he could get some fish and chips.

On the pier, Steve rummaged in his pockets and was pleased to discover that he had about a thirteen quid's worth of change. He wandered the length of the decking, scoffing his food and looking disinterestedly at the gaming machines and tourist tat. Having seen the North Laine hipsters earlier in the day, Steve was struck by how the folk strolling on the pier seemed a different breed altogether.

'So this is where all the square fuckers and out-of-towners come, then,' he thought. 'Time to find somewhere where a fella can get a dacent pint.'

He left the pier and walked westwards along the promenade until he came to the Fortune of War where groups of happy-looking twenty-somethings were congregating to enjoy a late afternoon drink in the sun.

Steve got a pint of Guinness in a plastic glass and took it onto the beach. He found a spot as far away from the gaggles of students and day-trippers as he could find, sat down on the pebbles and feasted on the view.

So here he was; a Mod sitting all on his lonesome on Brighton beach. Just like the part in *Quadrophenia* when Jimmy comes back to the scene of an earlier triumph only to find desolation and a drug-fuelled identity crisis. Only Steve didn't feel like that. Despite everything he'd been through, with the taste of Guinness in his mouth and the sunshine on his face, he felt pretty good. He liked the way the light was catching the sea, he liked the sound of seagulls and boozy laughter and the smell of deep-fried doughnuts. Just as he knew that he liked three-button jackets with narrow lapels, The Small Faces, booze, George Best and good-looking brunettes with bobbed hairstyles, in that moment he realised with total certainty that he liked Brighton.

11

'Oi!, wakey wakey. You're gonna have to get used to early mornings, boss... the guv'nor will be expecting some punctuality and hard graft on your first day before he decides if he'll keep you on.'

A mug of tea was placed at Steve's bedside as he yawned and mumbled his thanks to Bobby.

'Really appreciate this, mate... I won't let ye down. I know you've stuck yer neck out for me sayin' I'm a good worker 'n all... I could be a useless numpty for all you know.'

'C' mon boss, remember the shipyard workers who built the Titanic... you Belfast boys are made of pure grit, at least that's what my old man never tired of telling me, even though I heard from my uncle that he was always sneaking off to the bookies when he should have been grafting.'

Steve chuckled as he reached for his mug of tea.

'Well no worries on that front, mate ...wouldn't know one end of a horse from another but I've done plenty of casual labouring in my time... not too casual though, honest.'

'Glad to hear it, boss... now get into those work clothes that I've left out for you... gotta leave in ten minutes.'

The job was in Brunswick Square, only a few minutes walk from Bobby's flat. They both grabbed a takeaway bacon sandwich and coffee on the way and were there in good time for the eight 'o clock start.

With bright sunshine and the vivid blueness of the sea and the sky enhancing the scene, Steve was impressed with the location. The elegant Regency terraces exuded class and seemed to him to be every bit as exotic as anything he imagined the Mediterranean might have to offer. It felt like a far cry from the North Belfast backstreet that he'd run away from.

The building was being renovated by a local property developer whose long-term aim was to turn it into his own luxury home. In the seventies, the place had been converted into flats and many of the grand rooms had been fitted with lower ceilings to make them easier and cheaper to heat.

Steve's first task was to help Bobby rip the ceilings down on the top floor to reveal the original features. It was a filthy job and the pair wore protective masks to stop them choking on the dust.

Steve was true to his word about being a grafter, eager to prove to Bobby that his faith in him was justified. They worked without a break until one o'clock when Bobby offered to do the day's sandwich run.

'I fancy a cheese and ham baguette myself, boss. Yourself?'

'Aye, that'll do rightly for me too. A can o' Coke and a Mars Bar too, please.'

While Bobby was away sorting out their lunch, Steve rested himself against the wall on the hallway outside the room they were gutting. He liked the feeling of knowing that the lunch he was about to devour was well-earned. An Ulster Presbyterian work ethic had been drummed into him since childhood and the rebellious streak that he'd developed from adolescence onwards had done little to shake off the conditioning.

Steve was lightly dozing when he heard footsteps coming up the stairs and shouted a greeting to Bobby.

'I tell ye what, mate… I'm fuckin' starvin'… hope them baguettes are king-sized bastards …'

Steve rubbed his dirty hands against his jeans in anticipation but when he looked up, it wasn't Bobby standing at the top of the stairs. It was a vision of Mod elegance that made him gasp in admiration.

Facially, the guy resembled a younger Clint Eastwood, with small piercing eyes but with a sharper haircut that anything Steve had ever seen on Clint. His dark blue mohair suit looked like it had been painted onto his slim athletic frame and consisted of a three-button box jacket with one inch side vents and tight, narrow trousers tapering onto an immaculate pair of black Cuban heels. The ensemble was completed by a silk paisley shirt with button-down collars.

Steve felt like giving him a round of applause but instead, nervously blurted out a compliment.

'Hey man, really dig the threads!'

The be-suited guy walked slowly came forward with a forced-looking smile and Steve quickly stood up to greet him. He held out his hand for Steve to shake.

'I'm Anthony Cubitt.'

'Hi Anthony, I'm Steve …just been guttin' one of the rooms up here. I'm guessin' this is your gaff, then?'

As Steve talked he could feel Cubitt's grip on his hand get tighter. He stared straight into Steve's eyes, unblinkingly.

'Listen, bogtrotter. I don't give a damn what your name is or what unskilled task you're undertaking. Understand this. Don't ever address me in that vulgar manner again. In fact, don't assume that you are in a position to converse with me in any way whatsoever. Just get on with whatever inconsequential drudgery you're involved in and keep your mouth shut when I'm around. As far as I'm concerned, the likes of you are scum.'

The bone-crushing grip on Steve's hand kept intensifying until his eyes watered. Looking pleadingly into Cubitt's icy-blue eyes, Steve was in little doubt that the man was psychotic. He was on the verge of crying out in pain when Bobby's appearance on the scene disturbed Cubitt's concentration and he released Steve's hand. Without a word, Cubitt turned around, brushed past Bobby as if he wasn't there and walked straight down the stairs.

When he was sure Cubitt was out of earshot, Bobby asked Steve what had occurred.

'Please boss, don't tell me that you said something to annoy the Ace Face.'

'Ace Face? What are ye on about? And what's the crack with all that posh lingo he comes out with?'

'Ace Face is the nickname that the boys came up with 'cos of the Mod clobber. Not that we'd ever let him get wind of that. The snooty voice is just something that he's worked on 'cos I've heard on good authority that his dad was a street-cleaner from Worthing.'

'But he has to be gay, yeah?' said Steve. 'That theatrical manner 'n all… camp as fuck eh?'

Bobby snorted. 'Don't you fucking believe it. He's a proper shag merchant but only with industrial strength condoms apparently. He's a hygiene freak on top of everything else. But the point is, boss, I know you're enjoying the novelty of being in groovy, happening Brighton-by-the-sea but there's some dark stuff that can go on in this town that would make that mugging the other night look like a picnic… believe me, you really don't want to get on the wrong side of Anthony Cubitt.'

Steve laughed nervously.

'C'mon Bobby, I know he seemed like a bit of a nutter 'n all but surely it's just a bit of an act… tryin' to cultivate an image for himself or somethin'.'

'Okay, I'll spell it out for you, boss. He's done time for GBH and manslaughter, there seems to be an unfortunate tendency for his business rivals to have nasty unexplained accidents and the last judge to send him down described him as evil incarnate. Yeah, he's got an image alright.'

12

The rest of the week passed without incident at Brunswick Square and there was no sign of Cubitt as Steve and Bobby kept up their work-rate and made a good impression on the foreman. On Friday afternoon at knocking-off time, Steve was handed £300 in twenties and tens.

'Right, there's only one thing for it on a Friday afternoon at five' said Steve as he handed Bobby a fifty for the week's rent. 'C'mon, let's go and get fuckin' blocked!'

Bobby shook his head.

'Steady on, boss. I'd normally be right with you but to-night's different. We should go home, get washed and fed and then prepare ourselves for a quality night out.'

'Yer gettin' me excited here, Bobby. What's so special about tonight that I have to delay the gratification of gettin' a lovely pint o' stout down my neck?'

'Don't wanna spoil the surprise, boss. C'mon, let's get out of this filthy clobber and show the women of Brighton how well we can scrub up.'

Steve had a blue and white striped t-shirt identical to one that he'd seen worn by Brian Jones from The Rolling Stones in a 1965 photo. He ironed the creases out and when he pulled on his white Levis and a pair of tan desert boots to complete the outfit, he went to look at himself in the full-length mirror in the bathroom. As he fussed with his hair, he wasn't under any illusions that he was devastatingly handsome but he still thought he looked pretty sharp.

'That'll do rightly,' said Steve, winking at his reflection. Bobby knocked at the bathroom door.

'Oi, Belfast boy! Time to get a move on.'

13

It was a mild evening and the pair took a slow stroll along Upper North Street and then onto Clifton Terrace where Bobby wanted to show Steve what were, for his money, the most desirable houses in Brighton.

'This is where all the swanky merchants would have lived in Victorian times, boss. Just imagine having your bedroom on the top floor of one of these gaffs… views over the town and across the sea.'

Steve could smell lavender on the breeze from the residents' private park across the road from where they were walking.

'Yeah, there's bigger and more expensive houses all over the town but there's just something about this place… it's peaceful …ya know what I mean, boss?'

Steve tried picturing himself living somewhere like Clifton Terrace with a family of his own. It was a sweet dream but he felt slightly pathetic when he caught himself envisaging Jeanie as being part of it.

'Never mind how the other half lives Bobby, I'm dyin' o' thirst here. Where's this pub ye reckon I'll like, then?'

'Five minutes away, boss…almost there.'

14

Steve knew that the Heart and Hand was his kind of boozer from the moment he walked in. It looked like somebody's 1970s living room with fading décor to match, *Louie Louie* by The Kingsmen was on the jukebox and the place was packed with indie kids, ageing rockers and a smattering of Mods. He also noticed a sufficient quota of females to reassure him that it wasn't one of those male-dominated pubs where the atmosphere would be getting more testosterone-charged and lairy as last orders approached.

Bobby went to the bar and came back with two pints of Harvey's.

'So what's this gear you're expecting me to drink, then? Looks like cold tea with a bit o' froth on top.'

'Don't be a philistine, Belfast boy. This stuff is Sussex nectar… I can't take you on a night out in Brighton without you sampling some of the local ale.'

Steve took a sup while eyeing Bobby suspiciously.

'Well, I guess its just about drinkable… cheers mate.'

At the table next to the jukebox, a trendy-looking young couple were beckoning Bobby to join them.

'They're okay, boss,' Bobby whispered as they walked over. '… more acquaintances than friends but at least we've got a seat now.'

Bobby introduced the couple to Steve.

'Alright there Josh, how's it going? Nice to meet ye, Emily.'

Steve got a cold fish handshake from Josh and a faint, indifferent smile from Emily.

For the next couple of rounds, Steve found himself left out of the conversation as the pair prattled on to Bobby about their latest partying exploits and various Brighton scenesters that he'd never heard of while taking turns to go to the toilet more often than Steve thought was usually necessary.

'Ah, I geddit,' he thought. 'They're on the oul' devil's dandruff… instant arsehole powder.'

When it was his turn to get a round in, Steve quickly necked a double Jamesons at the bar before returning with pints for himself and Bobby and Tuacas for Josh and Emily, which were accepted without thanks.

Buoyed by booze and tired of being ignored, Steve decided that it was down to him to make the effort.

'So how do you folk know Bobby, then?'

With eyes that seemed to be scanning the pub to see if there was anyone more cool to talk to, Josh replied in a bored monotone.

'Just from being around clubs… I've DJ-ed at a couple of nights when Bobby's band were doing a set.'

'Nice one, mate. You DJ full-time then?'

Josh rolled his eyes.

'You'll find that DJ-ing in Brighton is usually a sideline except for the lucky few. I've got a day-job as a web designer.

Work's a bit scarce in Brighton so we're both commuting to London. Means getting up at six every morning but the money's good.'

'Don't know if I'd fancy that, Josh. Haulin' yer arse up there every mornin' with all them sour-faced gits on the train and I bet ye don't get back til about nine at night. No harm to ye but I couldn't be arsed with all that caper.'

The couple exchanged an embarrassed look. Emily piped up defensively.

'Well it works for us. We've got a great flat in Kemp Town with a sea view and the quality of life in Brighton is just fab. Really creative vibe here and everyone's so chilled.'

Steve laughed.

'I tell ye what love. If I was keepin' up that commutin' ballix I'd be chilled as fuck. I'd be walkin' around like a zombie on valium.'

With the couple starting to look ill-at-ease having to converse with a slightly drunk and opinionated working-class Irishman, Bobby thought it was time to change the subject.

'So Josh, been to any good gigs lately?'

'Saw one of the best I've been to in years. Billy Bragg played the Dome and....'

Steve butted in.

'Ach for fuck's sake ye don't like Billy Bragg do ye? All that batin' ye over the head with a placard preachy shite. He's just one of them fellas that gives it all of the man-of-the-people crack and ye can just tell that he's a self-serving egotistical fucker. Boy I hate that big-nosed cunt.'

Emily clunked her glass down on the table.

'I really would prefer it if you didn't use that word. I find it really offensive.'

'Not as offensive as some big-nosed, tone-deaf fucker singin' one of his dirgey fuckin' songs for a bunch o' smug middle-class twats.'

Emily reached for their coats.

'Let's go Josh.'

Steve took another swig of his pint and waved the angry couple goodbye, affecting a grating Home Counties accent.

'See ya guys. Have a lovely chilled-out evening, ya? Missing you already.'

As they watched the pair leave, Steve and Bobby got back to their pints and said nothing for the duration of Buffalo Springfield's *For What it's Worth* which had just come on the jukebox. As the tune faded, Bobby ended the conversational lull.

'Don't you think you were being a bit harsh there, boss?'

Steve grinned.

'Well mate, back in Belfast before the ceasefire, we'd have identified snattery wankers like them as bein' legitimate targets. I think I let them off lightly there. On another night I'd have been tempted to get the oul' Kalashnikov out and go for their kneecaps.'

Bobby shook Steve's hand and laughed.

'Indeed. Nice work, boss. Now let's quit this crazy scene, daddio. It's time for the main event… I'll call a taxi.'

15

As the taxi made its way through Kemp Town, Steve surveyed the goings-on under the street lights…butch-looking gays snogging passionately outside The Bulldog pub, a transvestite attempting to look feminine as he tottered along drunkenly in high heels, a wired-looking junkie hassling a young couple at a cash machine… it all held a seedy glamour in his newcomer's eyes. He turned his gaze back to the road ahead and could tell that the driver was intrigued by his passengers' appearance. He looked old enough to remember their 60s clothes from the first time around and had an impressive Elvis quiff streaked with grey.

'So is there a bit of a Mod do on tonight lads?'

'You guessed it, boss,' said Bobby. 'I take it you're of the Rocker fraternity?'

'Don't worry about that, lads. I'm a bit past scrapping on the beach. Anyway, you Mods have the edge in Brighton these days, dontcha? That psycho Cubitt is one of your lot aint he?'

'Don't think he's much of a team-player to be honest, boss. Anyway, I'm pleased to report that this particular

Mod disapproves of that head-case as much as you evidently do.'

The driver laughed darkly.

'I doubt that.'

'How come, boss?'

'You remember a few years back when an Italian restaurant in Shoreham got burnt to a crisp after Cubitt had been having a dispute with the management about owing him back-rent?'

Bobby nodded.

'I remember, boss. Three died in the fire, yeah?'

'That's right. And one of them was my brother's boy, trainee chef he was. Nineteen years old. A great lad he was too. Used to take him to the Albion every home game from when he was about eight. Death's too good for that scumbag Cubitt, I'm tellin' ya. He was behind the fire… everybody's knows it. If I had my way…'

The driver was making his grim pronouncement just as they approached the Hanbury Ballroom.

'Excuse me boss, this is us.'

The driver quickly pulled over as Bobby gave Steve a knowing look.

'Sorry lads. Thinkin' about that Cubitt bastard just gets me riled.'

'We understand boss… was telling Steve here all about that nutter the other day. Look, I've got six quid of shrapnel here… keep the change. And I'm really sorry to hear about what happened to your nephew.'

As the taxi drove off, Steve stood for a while to admire the venue's Indian-influenced architecture.

'Pretty impressive, eh?' said Bobby. 'Was originally a mausoleum for some Regency toffs.'

'Well I hope it's a bit more lively now, mate. Not many punters queuing up, are there?'

'Don't worry boss, it'll be packed inside. Let's get in there.'

16

At the entrance, where a thick-set Turkish bouncer stood with his shoulders thrust back purposefully as if he had mile-long queue to deal with, Steve could hear one his favourite tunes, *All About My Girl* by Jimmy McGriff, filtering through the doors.

'Check that, Bobby. Sounds like the DJs know their onions in this place.'

'You know you can rely on me to introduce you to the best nightspots, boss.'

The bouncer waved them through.

Once inside the club, Steve was impressed with its art-deco style, which was every bit as elegant as the exterior. Less impressive was the atmosphere. An aging couple in tight 60s clothes ill-suited to their middle-aged girth were behind the decks trying to exude cool but failing to do so. On the dancefloor, there were about six Mods nonchalantly shuffling around and checking out each other's moves. Judging by their non-Mod attire, the rest of the clientele looked liked they'd stumbled into the club by chance rather than design.

'Fuckin' hell Bobby, are ye sure this place aint still a mausoleum? Deadsville Arizona or wha'?'

'Patience, boss. It's bound to fill up soon so lets just get some beverages in and make the most of it, eh?'

Bobby went up to the bar and brought back a couple of pints. They took a seat close to where the DJs were gamely trying to build up some sort of momentum and watched the Mods' limp attempts at recreating the glory days of 1964. Then *Mississippi Delta* by Bobbie Gentry came on.

'C'mon boss, let's show 'em how it's done.'

Steve and Bobby flung themselves onto the dance-floor and joyously jumped around. The fun they were having made the other Mods' stiff posturing looked all the more lame. Gradually, the place got busier and Steve noticed that a trio of girls were making a point of dancing close to them.

None of the girls were particularly his type but one of them, a long-legged red-head in a tight-fitting blue dress, kept glancing his way. Flattered, Steve smiled at her and she responded with a saucy wink. For a while she danced with her back to him but the flirtation seemed to intensify when she began backing towards him, swinging her hips to the tune. An erection began stirring in his jeans and he pondered what his next move should be.

Then the DJ put on *I Can't Explain* by The Who and a tall, shaven-headed guy in a short-sleeved checked Ben Sherman shirt pushed his way through the crowd until he was dancing around the three girls. He then wrapped his arms around the red-head's waist. She turned round and kissed him passionately. Meanwhile, one of the other girls was whispering in Bobby's ear and stroking his arm. Bobby smirked at Steve as he moved his hand onto the girl's waist and drew her closer to him as they danced. Steve suddenly wasn't in the mood for dancing any more and sauntered off for another beer.

At the bar, a few rugger-bugger types were waving twenties to try to get the attention the bar staff but Steve's more under-stated approach got him served first and he ordered a pint of Becks.

'Only have that in bottles, is that okay?' said the barmaid.

'Aye, that'll do rightly, put a couple of them in a pint glass, thanks.'

She brought back the pint of beer and charged him seven pounds. Steve handed her the cash with a grimace and walked back towards the dance-floor muttering 'fuckin' rip-off' under his breath.

The supposed big night out in what was still an alien environment to Steve hadn't lived up to the build-up and as Bobby looked like he was getting lucky with the girl on the dance-floor, Steve felt a self-pitying sense of loneliness creep over him. The atmosphere hadn't improved much and he decided that his options were to either cut his losses and split, or stay and get more drunk. He decided on the latter and lined up a double Jack Daniels for when he'd finished his pint.

Out on the dance-floor, the rugger buggers were jumping around and spilling drinks over each other to the strains of *You Really Got Me* while about a dozen new arrivals were weaving their way towards the bar. One of them looked familiar.

'Sal!'

The girl who Steve had met on his first night in Brighton was sporting a polka-dot dress and had arranged her hair into a 60s beehive. She looked great. She came over and greeted him with a hug.

'Hey Steve, should have guessed you'd have turned up for a Mod night.'

Steve's heart sunk when he saw that a tall, sullen-looking rock 'n roller in skinny jeans with a trilby hat perched on the back of his head was lingering alongside her. He looked a little familiar and Steve realised that he'd noticed him when he'd explored the North Laine area the day after his arrival in Brighton. At first glance he thought he'd spotted Pete Doherty hanging around at the entrance of a tattoo parlour with his bohemian chums, smoking a fag. Up close, Steve noticed the crow's feet and flecks of grey hair. He may have been clad in teenage indie kid clothes but the guy had to be in his late thirties.

'Steve, this is Rich. Remember I told you he used to be in a band with Bobby?'

The two lads exchanged an awkward handshake and Steve felt sure that Rich was giving him a dirty look.

'Bobby's over there,' said Steve, gesturing towards the area nearest the DJs. 'You might find he's a bit preoccupied though.'

'Think I'll go over and say hi anyway,' said Rich. 'The fucker's owed me thirty quid for months. I'll be back in a jiff, Sal.'

He stroked Sal's arm territorially before strolling purposefully towards his debtor.

'He really fuckin' wants that money, eh?' said Steve.

Sal smiled.

'Yeah, tight bastard. Not one of his more endearing quali-
ties. I'm sure I'd have ditched him eventually if he hadn't
ditched me first.'

'Seems to me like you might be giving him another
chance.'

Sal looked at Steve apologetically.

'Steve, I really enjoyed the other night but it seemed to me
that you weren't gonna be around Brighton for long and you
didn't call me during the week so I just assumed you weren't
bothered.'

'It's been a mad week Sal and I've had a lot on my mind.
I really did want to see you again, honest. So have I blown it
then? What's the crack with Rich?'

Sal shook her head.

'I dunno. I've still got feelings for him so when he called
me out of the blue last night and asked if I fancied coming
along to the Hanbury, I just said yes 'cos I had nothing else
on. Maybe if he can get over his weakness for impression-
able 18-year-old art school chicks with a bad boy fixation, we
might have a chance, you never know.'

'You don't really owe me an explanation Sal. I just hope
he doesn't mess you around.'

Looking at her sweet face, Steve would have felt like kissing her again if he hadn't seen Rich striding back from the
dance-floor with an expression that seemed to confirm that he'd
retrieved his thirty quid and was smug in the knowledge that he
had a pretty girl's company guaranteed for the night too.

'C'mon Sal, lets get out of here,' said Rich. 'There's a
house party in Devonshire Place that'll be a lot livelier than

this place. They've set up decks and there's loads of booze apparently.'

'Free drink… your favourite two words in the English language, eh Rich? Alright then, let's skedaddle.'

Sal turned to Steve and gave him a peck on the cheek.

'Hey, it was nice to see you, Steve. Hopefully see you around again sometime.'

Rich put his arm around Sal and the pair walked off. Steve had hoped that Sal might make one last gesture to suggest that she was still interested in him and it was some consolation that she made a point of turning round to give him a parting smile as Rich held the exit door open for her.

'Oh dear, boss, looks like you should struck when the iron was hot the other night.'

Bobby had come up to the bar with his new conquest and was looking a lot more chipper than Steve was feeling.

'Aye, the luck of the Irish seems to have deserted me tonight, Bobby. But hey, the bar's still open. Fancy another wee swallee?'

'Nah, you're alright boss. Think me and Helen here are gonna hit the road.'

The girl gave Steve a coy little wave by means of introduction.

'Suit yerselves. I'm gonna get maself one more pint. I'll see ya back at the ranch later mate.'

The alcohol was anaesthetising the sense of lonesome-ness that Steve had felt earlier and he hadn't given up on the hope of finding someone to take home. As he lent on the bar, he looked to his left and started taking in the rear view of an elegant-looking brunette with hair cascading down her back who was chatting to a pair of female friends. She was wearing a slinky knee-length black dress that clung to her curves and emphasised the peachiness of her ass. Steve reckoned that if her face was anywhere near as attractive as the rest of her, she'd be a stunner. He pondered what sort of opening gambit he might make to get talking to her. He opted for something innocuous.

'Sorry to bother ye luv,' he said as he tapped the girl on the shoulder. 'Do ye know what time this gaff shuts at?'

His heart lurched when she turned round.

'Jeanie!'

17

Her hair and style of dress had changed radically but there was no mistaking those cheekbones, full lips and big brown eyes.

'Christ Almighty… Steve! What the hell are you doing here?'

Steve had prayed so long for this moment that the sight of Jeanie before him hardly seemed real. He could feel his voice trembling as he tried to keep his composure.

'I'm, uh… well, I just fancied getting away for a while. You know how it is Jeanie… anyway, I reckon it's you that has some explainin' to do.'

Jeanie looked at him impassively with a mildly bemused smile.

'Sometimes a girl just needs to spread her wings. Belfast was just doing my nut in, darlin'.'

So that was the best she could muster? All those months of misery and soul-searching, lying awake at night mulling over every possibility of where she could be and what might have become of her.

'Jesus, is that all you've got to say to me? For fuck's sake Jeanie, all you left me was that poxy note that explained fuck all and left me worried sick. I thought we had something together and next thing you do a fuckin' Lord Lucan act on me.'

Jeanie noticed that her companions were becoming all too aware of their lively exchange.

'Could you keep it down, Steve? I don't think we should be discussing this here'.

Her voice quietened to a whisper.

'Look darlin', I've been wanting to ditch these too all night, they've been boring the arse off me. I'll have a quick word then we can split. Okay?'

18

'Let's just find somewhere quiet where we can get a drink, okay?' Jeanie said brusquely as they walked along Marine Parade towards the Palace Pier.

Steve struggled to think of how he could get a conversation going as she moodily blew smoke rings from her Menthol cigarette.

Outside the Madeira Hotel, two girls in hen night fancy dress were sat on the pavement with one of them holding the other's hair back as she puked into a drain.

'Classy,' said Jeanie.

'Seen a lot worse in Belfast,' said Steve, '... at least she's keepin' the boke outta her mate's hair. That's showin' a lotta class in my book.'

'Yeah and using the drain's a nice touch too, very civic-minded,' added Jeanie.

They smiled at each other for the first time that night.

'Hey darlin', I've remembered somewhere we could get a late one,' said Jeanie. 'Place called The Fishbowl, just a couple of minutes away, okay?'

The bar was still busy at 2 am but they had little trouble getting served and managed to find a seat by the window upstairs. Looking at her in the dim candle light, Steve felt himself fall under the spell of Jeanie's beauty anew. He realised he barely cared what she had to say for herself. The fact that she was there right in front of him was all that mattered.

'So what's the story then, Jeanie? What was so bad about Belfast that you had to do a moonlight flit?'

Jeanie gave him a seductively wide-eyed look and sipped on her glass of red wine before replying.

'I don't know what you'll think of me if I tell you the truth, darlin'.'

'I can handle it.'

She set her glass down.

'You remember that nightclub where I used to work?'

'Aye, how could I forget a godforsaken meat-market like Temptations? All those flash wankers wavin' their cash around and tryin' to chat you up... and that sleazy posh-boy manager James Wilson always sniffin' around you.'

Around 2004, Temptations had been marketed relentlessly as an upmarket addition to the nightlife of a rejuvenated Belfast and moneyed urbanites flocked to the place in their droves while bohemians and inverted snobs like Steve and his Mod associates despised the place.

'What can I say, darlin'. A girl's gotta make a living. The problem was that the money was shit and one night Temptations was the operative word...'

She smiled enigmatically.

'Don't go all mysterious on me, Jeanie. Spill the beans.'

'Okay then. There was this backroom where James and the staff used to go for a little, y' know, late night pick-me-up after the punters had left and we'd cleared up.'

'You mean you'd be snorting coke into the wee small hours?'

'I guess sometimes we did, yeah.'

'So you got a bit of a coke problem that you didn't want me to know about and you had to get away to go into rehab? Christ, Jeanie, I'd have been able to handle that. I'm no moralist.'

Jeanie took a large gulp of wine before continuing.

'If only it was as simple as a spell in rehab, darlin'. The thing is, they kept a safe in the back room and when the boss was putting the night's takings away, he didn't realise that I wasn't so off my nut that I couldn't keep an eye on what combination he was using.'

Steve got the uneasy sense that he'd never really known this girl at all.

'So you're telling me that you're not a drug addict, you're just a thief. That's okay then.'

'No need to get sarky with me darlin'. Anyway, I thought you said you weren't a moralist.'

The same Presbyterianism that had instilled a work ethic in Steve also made him abhor dishonesty and he was finding it hard to reconcile this with the intense desire that Jeanie aroused in him.

'Just tell me how much you stole, Jeanie. If you're in the shit, I'd like to know how deep it is.'

A faint smirk appeared on her face before she replied.

'Twenty-five grand. Add half a kilo of coke and I'd guess I'm forty-five grand deep in shit, if that's the way you want to see it. So do you see now, darlin'? My leaving Belfast was nothing to do with how I felt about you.'

Steve looked in her eyes for signs of shame or regret but he didn't see any.

'Well I've told you now, Steve. Aren't you going to say anything?'

'What the fuck do you expect me to say? Well done, Jeanie, you're a criminal mastermind? So I'm guessin' when you fucked off, James Wilson must have gone straight to the peelers and told them who he thought the culprit was.'

Jeanie's calm façade no longer seemed convincing.

'Thing is, Steve, James was just the respectable public face of Temptations... it's the owner of the place I've got to be worried about and he wasn't the type to have much truck with the police. You might have heard of him, he came from round your way... a nasty piece of work called Trevor McCann.'

19

After blurting out a 'holy fuck!' that made a few heads turn round, Steve offered to go up to the bar for more drinks. He brought back two large Jamesons and proceeded to tell Jeanie all about his own run-in with Trevor McCann.

'Oh darlin', that's so awful… I know how close you were with Doug. I was fond of him too, he was such a lovely guy.'

The words seemed hollow when Steve remembered how cold Jeanie had been towards Doug; never making any effort to be civil to him whenever she'd stayed over at their house, but he tried not to dwell on that.

'Thanks Jeanie. What a fuckin' mess eh?'

She lent closer and held Steve's hand.

'Well let's just hope that being in Brighton is the best way of getting out of the mess for the both of us. C'mon, let's get out of here. There's a place I think you'd like to see just near here.'

Still holding his hand, Jeanie led Steve out of the pub and down East Street. Just past a row of shops, she stopped at a narrow alleyway.

'You know where this is, don't you?'

Steve smiled.

'Fuck! It's where Jimmy and Stef hid from the cops in Quadrophenia, isn't it?'

Jeanie gave him a sultry look that made him horny as hell.

'But they made good use of their time in there, didn't they? Do you want me to refresh your memory about how?'

She led Steve into the alley and they French-kissed with an intensity that made him feel dizzy. With her back against a wall, she took no time to reach for his cock while his left hand caressed the nipple of a bra-less breast.

'Fuck me Steve. Now!'

Jeanie deftly un-buckled Steve's jeans so they fell around his ankles. A night's drinking had done little to weaken the strength of his erection and she stroked his balls as he fingered her wet pussy. As usual, she had no knickers on under her dress and as he lifted her by her bare ass to straddle him, she put her arms around his shoulders and kissed him again. He'd always loved the feeling of her mouth against his.

'C'mon darlin', fuck me hard!'

'Christ Jeanie, you're beautiful…'

It was as if they were trying to devour each other as Steve thrust his cock in as deep as he could.

'Oh God, it feels like you've got bigger …. c' mon, harder darlin'. I want to feel you come inside me… oh sweet Jesus!'

20

Steve's head was still spinning as they walked back onto East Street.

'Hey Jeanie, can we sit down by the sea for a while?'

As they walked, she squeezed his hand and kissed him briefly on the cheek.

'I'd love to darlin' but I really should be getting home. I can pick up a taxi at the top of the street.'

'So when can I see you again?'

Jeanie stopped walking and looked at Steve pleadingly.

'Thing is darlin', my life is a little complicated at the moment and meeting up might be tricky.'

'You mean you're seeing someone.'

'I said it's complicated, Steve,' Jeanie snapped. 'Let's just leave it at that.'

'So am I gonna see you again or not?'

She let out an exasperated sigh.

'Okay Steve, I tell you what. Come and meet me at Waves Café on Madeira Drive next Sunday at three. There's a Mods and Rockers reunion thing happening and you'd be able to check out the scooters. There's no punch-ups any more, honest… they just admire each others bikes and shoot the breeze.'

Steve was gutted that she was being off-hand so soon after their love-making but he was determined to keep his composure.

'Sounds cool, I'll see you then. Or if you're ever around Lansdowne Place, give us a knock. Number 76… easy to re-member… year I was born 'n all.'

From the disinterested look in her eyes, he could tell that there was little chance of an impromptu visit anytime soon. They exchanged a brief kiss and Jeanie headed towards the queue of loud-talking drunks at the East Street taxi rank while Steve walked southwards towards the sea wondering what the hell had just happened.

21

Steve woke up to the sound of giggles and The Beach Boys'
Sunflower album coming from Bobby's bedroom. The previous night's encounter with Jeanie had left him feeling a
disorientating mix of dark anxiety and romantic longing.
He recalled Johnny Bell's warning that she was 'really
bad news' but still he knew that he would be counting the
days until the agreed meeting on Madeira Drive the next
weekend.

By the sounds of things, Bobby and Helen were enjoying a morning fuck so Steve decided to leave the flat to get
himself a Daily Mirror and a hangover-curing can of Pepsi
followed by a fry-up.

After popping into the newsagent, he strolled along
Church Road swigging his Pepsi until he came to Harry's
English Restaurant. It was a bit more posh than his usual
haunts but he fancied treating himself. He bagged a window
seat and settled down to read his paper. It was a habit he'd
got into since he was a teenager and as he skimmed through
pages of inconsequential tripe about reality TV shows and
drug-addled rock stars, he wondered why he bothered.

After the waitress took his order of a full English breakfast, Steve picked a copy of The Argus that the table's previous occupant had left behind. Steve found it hard to feel much interest in a threatened bin men's strike or the presentation of a cake to some pensioners but on Page 5, something caught his eye.

The headline read 'Cubitt's Parisian adventure' and next to it was a photo of the 'controversial local property developer' looking like a 1960s French movie star. The feature described how Cubitt had bought a derelict building near the centre of Paris and was in the process of transforming it into 'one of Europe's most exclusive hotels.'

'He is currently dividing his time between Sussex and France and is hoping to complete work on the hotel early next year,' the article continued, '… but as relatives of the victims of a fire at Giuseppe's restaurant in Shoreham continue their campaign to have the case re-examined by the police because they claim to have found conclusive proof of Cubitt's involvement in starting the blaze, his profile is likely to remain high.'

The rest of the paper enlightened Steve to some local architectural planning controversies and Brighton and Hove Albion's pre-season transfer activity and once he'd finished his breakfast, he decided that he fancied getting back to the flat and luxuriating in a bath.

When he returned, Bobby was sprawled out on the sofa watching a favourite edition of Soccer AM that he'd saved on Sky-plus.

'So where's the lovely lady then?' asked Steve. Bobby was struggling not to look smug.

'Think she needed to get home to recover from a night of Bobby-love. Poor girl was shagged senseless.'

'Spoken like a true gent, Bobby.'

Bobby turned back to the TV to look at a nubile girl in a Queens Park Rangers kit performing a cheesy dance routine to Jean Knight's *Mr. Big Stuff* with the show's presenter while groups of beer-bellied lads cheered them on.

'Go on boss, make us a brew eh?'

Steve went into the kitchen and returned with a teapot and a couple of mugs.

'Nice one,' said Bobby. 'So how did you get on last night after me and Helen left?'

'Well, let's see… apart from bumpin' into the Belfast girl who broke my heart and re-enactin' the sex scene from Quadrophenia, bit of a quiet one, really.'

Bobby turned the volume down on the TV.

'You're kiddin' me, yeah?'

'Nope.'

'For fuck's sake boss, spill the beans!'

Steve told Bobby all about Jeanie's disappearance the previous summer and their steamy reunion but decided to leave out the stuff about Trevor McCann. Bobby particularly seemed to relish the details of the quickie in the East Street alleyway.

'So she's a looker then, boss?'

'You could say that. Best lookin' girl I've ever got within a mile of. Imagine Wynona Ryder with Angelina Jolie's lips and you're almost there.'

'Fuckin' 'ell, boss. I'll be getting the horn again if you get me thinkin' about a knee-trembler with girl who looks like that. I'll be on the blower to Helen to get her over for another sesh. You don't have a photo of her, do ya?'

Steve looked sheepish.

'I know it's a bit pathetic, but I've always kept her photo in my wallet.'

He pulled the wallet out of his back pocket and handed the picture to Bobby.

'Her hair's grown a lot since then but she's as gorgeous as ever.'

Steve proudly looked to see Bobby's reaction.

'Please say you're just messin' with me.'

'Course I'm not. That's her, I swear. Stunning eh?'

Bobby solemnly handed him back the photo.

'I recognise her, boss. She's quite well-known about town.'

'What are ye tryin' to say here, Bobby? I hope you're not suggestin' that she's a slapper or somethin'.'

Bobby switched off the TV and looked straight at Steve.

'No, nothing like that… look, this is a fuckin' hard thing to tell you but you really need to know… the girl in that photo is Anthony Cubitt's woman.'

22

'I think we might need to put some crisis management into place here, boss.'

Bobby poured the tea out and handed one of the mugs to Steve.

'Well it's not like she's goin' to tell him, Bobby.'

'Of course not but Brighton's a small place… just takes one person at the Hanbury or the Fishbowl who recognises her to blab about it and it could be round the town like wildfire.'

'Yeah but no-one else knows about what happened in the alleyway… if Cubitt hears she was seen with me she could just say that I'm an old friend or somethin'.'

Bobby sighed.

'Look boss, we're talking about Anthony Cubitt here… this is not a reasonable man who'll be willing to listen to explanations about why his woman has been seen with another man… you need to get your head around this, boss… he'll want to inflict some serious damage on you if he finds out.'

Steve bristled.

'Look Bobby, why the fuck should I be runnin' scared of a jumped-up arsehole like him? And never mind what he'd do to me… if he laid a hand on Jeanie over this, I'd batter the cunt, I swear.'

'No offence boss, but you didn't look too tough when he gave you that bone-crushing handshake the other day.'

Steve gave Bobby the finger.

'Up yours, mate… the fucker just got me by surprise. You forget I'm from North Belfast… wankers like Cubitt would get eaten for breakfast by some of the hard men who are knockin' around where I grew up.'

Bobby gave Steve a conciliatory smile.

'Look boss, I don't doubt that Belfast might give you a bit of added grit compared to most of the airy-fairy ponces that live around this manor but you gotta understand, Cubitt is a bona fide one-hundred-per-cent certified psycho. Don't let the posh voice and the snazzy threads convince you otherwise.'

Steve reached for the teapot and topped up both their mugs.

'Alright then, so what's this crisis management you have in mind, Bobby?'

Bobby took a few sups of tea before replying.

'Okay, maybe I was being a bit melodramatic but as they say, forewarned is forearmed. Firstly, you need to stay well clear of her from now on. Secondly, I'm usually up-to-date on the Brighton gossip-mill so at the first hint that Cubitt's blowing a gasket over his woman, it's time for you to head straight home to Belfast, ya dig?'

Steve shook his head.

'No can do, mate …look, there's stuff I've been keepin' to myself since I got here. You've been a good friend to me from the word go so maybe now's as good a time as any to tell you the whole fuckin' saga …I wouldn't usually be up for hair-of–the-dog this time of day but I really think this needs to be discussed over a pint.'

23

Over three rounds of Guinness in a quiet corner at The Cooper's Cask, Bobby became fully au fait with Trevor and Donzo, the murder of Doug, paramilitary drug-dealing, the close-knit Belfast Mod scene and Jeanie's misdemeanours.

'Well I hope you feel better for telling me that 'cos I'm not sure if I feel better for knowing it… god bless ya, boss, I think you've been keeping it together better than I would have.'

'Appearances can be deceptive, Bobby. Believe you me, I've been feelin' anxious as fuck and all that shite never stops whirrin' through my head. I really miss havin' that peace of mind when you can just switch off and appreciate the simple things… I think I've understood for the first time why people turn to Diazepam and shit like that… '

'Well let's just stick to booze, boss. One more round? It's my shout.'

While Bobby was at the bar, Steve looked at all the carefree young people enjoying a Saturday afternoon drink. Practically all of them looked healthily middle-class and trendy and he reckoned that the worst trauma any of then would have been through was mummy and daddy not getting funds into their bank account quick enough for their next term at 'Uni'.

He overheard the group at the next table loudly enthusing about Eddie Izzard's latest DVD and quoting lines from it. He felt like shouting 'shove yer smug, whimsical, self-conscious English bullshit right up yer fuckin' holes' but he managed to stop himself.

When Bobby brought the pints back to the table he could see the look of contempt on Steve's face.

'C'mon boss,' he whispered. 'They're harmless enough… live and let live 'n all'.

Steve looked slightly ashamed.

'Yeah, you're right. If I start losin' sight of stuff like that I'm lettin' bastards like Trevor and Cubitt rule the day.'

Steve clinked glasses with Bobby.

'Cheers mate. Here's to peace, love and understanding, eh?'

24

Back at work, the hard graft made Steve feel more upbeat. There had been no sign of Anthony Cubitt since their initial encounter and later in the week, he overheard one of the builders saying that the 'Ace Face' had just flown over to Paris and was going to be there for a week working on the new hotel project. This made Steve feel a little more at ease but there was still the nagging worry that someone might have seen him with Jeanie and blabbed about it. In particular, he worried that the girls she'd been with at the Hanbury might be embroiled with Cubitt too.

When the weekend came, Bobby was keen to hook up with Helen and although they had a few pints together after work on Friday, by Saturday night, Steve found himself alone in the flat while Bobby had been invited round to his new girl's flat for dinner. Come Sunday morning, loneliness was creeping in. Steve tried to keep himself occupied with Sunday papers and TV but the temptation to ignore Bobby's advice to keep away from Jeanie was proving too much when he knew he could see her again if he just got himself over to Madeira Drive by three o'clock.

By lunchtime he was truly bored with the papers and when he switched on the TV to find the *Eastenders* omnibus edition about to start, the lure of meeting Jeanie became irresistible.

The sun was shining and as he walked along Western Road, Steve looked through the windows of the restaurants and cafes full of smiling, contented faces. He was beguiled by Brighton life but wondered if he'd ever truly feel part of it. Outside Waitrose, the same beggar who'd been there the night he got mugged was playing a tin whistle badly and Steve chucked him another couple of quid. 'Good for the oul' karma, as the hippies say,' he thought.

When he reached the seafront via West Street, the promenade was choc-a-bloc with day-trippers and on Madeira Drive, Steve felt a glow of pride when he saw a cavalcade of Mods imperiously glide past on their gleaming scooters. Outside Volks Tavern, a few other Mods had parked up and were standing around chatting and smoking. Some of the middle-aged ones looked a bit ridiculous sporting haircuts and tight-fitting clothes more suited to skinny teenagers but there were younger converts too and seeing excitable-looking, fresh-faced kids being as sharp and immaculately-dressed as the original 60s innovators made Steve smile. Mingling with the Mods was a bunch of hairy, beer-drinking bikers standing next to their pristine Triumphs and Harley Davidsons. The atmosphere was genial, as if a shared love of two-wheeled transport had finally superseded the violent rivalry of yore.

The good weather had drawn people outdoors so Steve had no problem getting a window seat in the café. He pulled a Bukowski paperback out of his back pocket and supped his cappuccino. Jeanie had never arrived on time for any of their meetings in the past so he was expecting to be waiting for a while.

After twenty minutes or so, he was getting quite engrossed with Bukowski's drunken escapades when there was a rap on the window. Jeanie flashed him a killer smile. She had her hair tied back in a pony-tail and was wearing a Breton shirt and navy blue ski-pants. A simple type of retro chic that put Steve in mind of Audrey Hepburn in *Funny Face*. She breezed in and pecked him on the cheek.

'Sorry I'm a wee bit late darlin'. You want another coffee?'

She brought back two cappuccinos and slinked into the seat next to Steve.

'So how's my favourite Mod? Bet you're enjoying seeing your compadres in all their finery?'

'Yeah, makes me feel the loss of my scooter a bit more deeply though… fuckin' Trevor and Donzo …'

She stroked his arm and smiled sympathetically.

'There there, darlin'. Sure it won't be long before you've got another cool set of wheels. I've got nice memories of our wee excursions together… remember that weekend in Portstewart?'

Six times in one night. It was Steve's all-time shagging record.

'Yeah, how could I forget?'

As Steve recalled possibly the top selection from his wank jukebox, a trio of fat daytrippers in Chelsea shirts with loud cockney accents barged into the cafe.

'I'm fakkin' dyin' for some chips… oi, Gaz, you get 'em… I've been gettin' the beers in all fakkin' afternoon, you tight-arsed slag.'

Jeanie grimaced.

'I think this is our cue to leave, darlin'. I'm not enjoying the ambience any more. Let's go for a stroll in the sun, eh?'

Back in the sunshine, the young Mods Steve had been observing earlier were getting interviewed by a presenter that he recognised from a BBC2 arts programme. Steve and Jeanie quickly shuffled out of the way when they realised they were within range of the cameraman's lens. Jeanie linked arms with Steve and led him along the pavement towards Brighton Marina.

'There's a lovely walk if we keep going along this way, darlin'… the tourists don't know about the undercliff path so we'll be able to avoid the riff-raff.'

Steve wondered what Jeanie was on about when an Asda supermarket and an ugly expanse of concrete came into view but once they got beyond that and walked alongside dramatic white cliffs with a dazzling sea to their right, he could see what she meant.

A pair of laughing kids holding fishing nets skipped along as a purposeful-looking lycra-clad cyclist flew past in the opposite direction. With the sun in her face, Jeanie looked content. Steve began to wonder why the chaos and drama in her life never seemed to cause her any concern. When she turned to look at him, she noticed the questioning look in his eyes.

'Penny for 'em, darlin'.'

Steve kicked a stone along the path as he walked.

'Ach I was just wonderin' why you always seem no non-chalant about everythin'... it's like whatever shite happens, ye don't have a care in the world.'

Jeanie stopped walking and unlinked her arm from Steve's.

'Well I just thought we were having a perfectly pleasant stroll in the sun. Why should I be bothered about anything?'

Steve tried to hold Jeanie's hand again but she withdrew it from his grasp.

'Look Jeanie, I didn't mean to bug ye, it's just that I find you pretty hard to figure out sometimes. And ye might as well know, I know about you and Cubitt... I showed a friend your photo and he knew who you were.'

An elderly couple had just walked past and Jeanie waited until they were out of earshot before replying to Steve.

'How fucking dare you.'

'Look, I couldn't just pretend that ...'

'I said how fucking dare you, Steve. You don't own me and it's my business who I see.'

'So what about the other night, then?'

Jeanie cackled.

'Oh get a grip, Steve. A quick drunken shag up an alley-way does not a relationship make.'

Steve's precious memory of a sensuous moment was shattered.

'Thanks Jeanie. It's good to know it meant as much to you as it did to me. But I just don't get it... I'm under no illusions about my status in life but fuckin' Cubitt... how could you ever get mixed up with a psycho bastard like that?'

Jeanie began walking away.

'Answer me, Jeanie. How could you be with such an evil scumbag?'

Jeanie turned round and glared at him.

'Okay, you asked for it Steve. Because he's a real man, not some day-dreaming backstreet loser. Oh, and he's the best fuck I've ever had. I come every time with him and if you really want to know, I always had to fake it with you. It's hard to get too aroused by someone that deep down, you just feel sorry for.'

Steve flinched like a dog that had just been kicked.

'Ach please, Jeanie…'

All he could was stand and watch as she faded from view in the hazy sunshine.

25

Steve spent the next few weeks in a fug of despair. Work at the Regency house provided a welcome distraction. A dividing wall needed removing in one of the larger rooms on the second floor and Steve relished taking out his frustration on it. One Friday afternoon, as the rest of the workers started slacking off as the weekend beckoned, Bobby felt compelled to have a word.

'For fuck's sake slow down a bit, boss. You're showing the rest of us up.'

'Hard graft is the best therapy I know, Bobby, but maybe yer right.'

He put the sledgehammer down.

'Okay, I'll pace myself so that this wee job takes me up 'til knockin' off time. And ye better be up for goin' for a pint instead of buggerin' off to see yer girl again.'

'Alright boss. The gaffer's gonna let us get off early today so Cooper's Cask at four o'clock it is. You never know your luck… there might be some nice chicks around to admire those bulging biceps you've been growing lately.'

Bobby was good to his word and by five, the pair already had a couple of pints under the belt as the barmaid brought two home-made quarter-pound beef burgers with chunky fries to their table.

'Could ye get us another couple of pints, luv?' said Steve.

With their meals quickly devoured and a fresh pint put in front of them, Steve and Bobby lent back contentedly and watched the pub fill up with the Friday night crowd. Bobby knew all about the ill-fated meeting with Jeanie and its effect on Steve's mood but they'd avoided the subject until half way through the third pint.

'So boss, hope that encounter was enough to draw a line under the Jeanie saga. Time you got out there and found yourself a nice easy-going Brighton girl who won't fuck with your mind or put you in mortal danger.'

'Yeah yeah, I know mate but the other thing I've been worryin' about is that I don't have a baldy notion what's been happenin' back home. Like have Trevor and Donzo been tryin' to find out where I am or have the peelers been on their case or wha'?'

'Maybe its time you called one of your home-town confidants to find out how the land lies, boss.'

Steve nodded.

'Aye, sure I got maself a wee pay-as-you-go job the other day. About time I made use of it.'

After another pint, they made for home so that Bobby could wash and change before he went to meet Helen while Steve was happy to veg out on the sofa. Around seven, he heard Bobby shout 'Have a nice evening, boss' as he left the flat. With the place to himself, he finally felt ready to put in a call to Johnny Bell to see if there was any significant news from Belfast. He called Johnny's landline number, which he knew by heart.

'Steve, is that you? Good fuckin' job you called, hombre. Can't say for sure if it'll have got back to Trevor but all our crew know that you and Jeanie are in Brighton.'

Steve sat bolt upright on the sofa.

'Please say yer rakin' me Johnny. You didn't let it slip did ya?'

'Blame the power of television. Some feature on The Culture Show last week about Mods. They were interviewin' these guys in Brighton and there yez were standin' around in the background, as large as life. There was no mistakin' it. Let's face it hombre, the pair of ye are quite distinctive.'

'Oh fuck.'

Steve remembered how he and Doug had once been caught in a close-up shot of fans during a televised Northern Ireland international match. He'd lost count of the amount of people who'd mentioned to him that they'd seen it.

'Well there's fuck all I can do about that now. Can ye tell the crew to try an' keep a lid on it? I mean, I can't see Trevor and Donzo bein' regular Culture Show viewers, can you?'

'Maybe so hombre but Belfast is a village where a lot of talkin' gets done and I could no more stop our lot gassin' than ye could have stopped Geordie Best drinkin'.'

Steve continued chatting with Johnny for a while but as panic gripped him, he couldn't concentrate much on what was being said. He ended the call and began desperately weighing up his options. He had a few hundred quid and could possibly get a flight out of the country but would have little left to survive on once the fare was paid. He thought of his cousin in

Scotland again. Surely he wouldn't mind putting him up for a couple of nights? Steve went straight to his bedroom and began throwing all his gear into his holdall. It was decided. He'd get a train to London and then get himself on the overnighter to Edinburgh.

Steve dashed down the stairs and walked out the front door on to Lansdowne Place. At the same time he met the night-time air, his jaw was met by a fist.

'Long time no see, fuckhead.'

Steve tumbled to the pavement, and after kicking him in the guts, his assailant grabbed him by the scruff of the neck and bundled him into the back seat of a black BMW.

26

'**Nice wee town** you've landed in, fruity boy. Is that why ye moved here? Plenty of other fruits around by the looks of things.'

The car was gliding along Western Road and Trevor had noticed groups of revellers who were already getting in the swing of things for the Gay Pride march the following day.

'Fuckin' freaks… aye, you must be right at home here with all the other weirdoes.'

As Trevor gawped out the car window, Steve's main view was the back of Donzo's shaven head with 'For God and Ulster' tattooed on his neck.

Trevor started chuckling.

'What gets me is that ye made it so fuckin' easy for us. My manager at Temptations tells me you've been advertisin' yerself on BBC2 then all I have to do is put in a few calls to fellas I know in the buildin' trade over here 'cos I knew rightly that's the only kinda work you'd be able to get. Even more easy peasy 'cos Donzo's uncle's workin' as a site foreman in the same fuckin' town and was able to put the feelers out nae bother.'

Donzo chipped in.

'Thing is, its yer dopey fuckin' haircut that was the dead giveaway when we started askin' around. If you'd shaved yer oul' bap like I do, no fucker would have noticed ye.'

Donzo indicated right and turned down Waterloo Street towards the seafront. Steve was still in a daze from their assault on him but managed to splutter out a question.

'Where the fuck are youse takin' me?'

Trevor smirked.

'Thought ye might enjoy a wee trip along the coast. Me and Donzo have been gettin' to know this part of the world the last couple 'o days and there's a nice wee spot called Beachy Head we thought ye might like to see.'

27

It was the first time Steve had seen the Seven Sisters cliffs but the view from Beachy Head was instantly recognisable to him because of the spectacular aerial footage in his favourite movie.

'Thanks for taking me here, lads. It's one of the locations from Quadrophenia that I've always really wanted to visit. It's where Jimmy rode his scooter along the cliff-edge… fuckin' class!'

'Don't waste yer time tryin' to be a smartarse, ye sarky wee slabber' snapped Trevor. 'Yer not funny and I'm not fuckin' interested in hearin' about yer Quadro Fenian or any other kind of Fenian. Just keep movin', fuckhead'.

Trevor and Donzo kept close behind Steve and whenever he was sure no-one in the vicinity was looking, Donzo shoved Steve forward with a fierce punch in the back. Steve let out a loud grunt.

'Keep the fuckin' noise down and don't even think about makin' a dash for it,' said Trevor. 'Donzo may be a big fella but he can out-run any bastard I know.'

Looking down on the five hundred foot drop below, Steve saw a lighthouse. He fleetingly thought of all the lives it must have saved but knew it wouldn't be any use in helping to save his.

'It's a sad oul' story, aint it Donzo?'

'Sure is, Trevor.'

Steve turned around to face them. The two fat, red-faced, tattooed Ulstermen looked incongruous against the gentle rural Sussex backdrop. Donzo was wearing a Glasgow Rangers top while Trevor had squeezed his bulk into a beige summer suit from Next.

"Aye, it's an awful shame, Donzo' continued Trevor. 'Poor wee fella from Belfast is so upset about his bum-chum dyin' that he decides to top himself at a lonely spot far away from home. Happens all the time... I hear there were nearly twenty suicides here last year. What the oul' Belfast Telegraph would call a 'grim statistic' eh?"

Steve could see an elderly couple walking their Scottish terrier nearby and thought of shouting something to them but they were soon out of view.

'But before we conclude this wee bit o' business, there's also the matter of that wee whore-bag that you were seen with when ye got clocked on TV,' said Trevor.

'I suppose ye know we've got an issue with her too so ye better fuckin' tell us where she is.'

Donzo licked his lips.

'Aye, she's a wee ride too and we'll have a good oul' rattle at her before we dole out the real punishment. Reckon we'll have the bitch both ways, eh Trevor?'

Steve bristled.

'For a start, you're fuckin' wastin' yer time there 'cos I don't have a notion where she lives and ...'

Steve took a deep breath.

'… and if you ever lay a hand on her, you're fuckin' dead.'

Trevor and Donzo looked at each other and laughed loudly in unison.

'Yer man's a geg, aint he Donzo? A real fuckin' joker.'

It was then that Steve chose his moment. He swiftly swung his boot into Donzo's bollocks and when Trevor lurched towards him, Steve managed to land a crunching right hook straight into his throat. As the pair groaned, Steve stood at the cliff's edge with the sea behind him and beckoned to them.

'C'mon ta fuck ye fat bastards. I'll batter the pair of youse'.

With Donzo still writhing in pain, Trevor came at Steve with both fists clenched.

'If you think some fruity fucker like you can take us boys on, you're a bigger head-the-ball than I thought,' he croaked.

Trevor swung at him but as he did, Steve took a vicious kick at his ankle like the dirtiest football tackle ever.

Trevor stumbled sideways and stuck his arms out to try to break the fall but ended up diving right over the edge of Beachy Head. With screams ringing in their ears, Steve and Donzo were left facing each other.

'Not so fuckin' brave without a baseball bat, are ye fatboy?'

Steve maintained his stance on the cliff's edge and flicked Donzo a fuck-off V-sign.

'C'mon, ye scummy fat fucker. Do ye wanna end up like Trevor or do ye fancy yer chances?'

Steve began to tease Donzo, dancing around in a circle like Muhammad Ali and daring him to take him on. Disorientated

and dizzy, Donzo kept lurching towards him until he unwit-
tingly ended up on the precarious spot where Steve had just
been standing.

Still cringing with pain, Donzo lumbered forward away
from the cliff's edge. With his shiny bald head glistening in
the evening sunshine and rolls of flab wobbling underneath
his Rangers top, he didn't look quite so menacing in the wake
of Trevor's demise. Tears were streaming down his face.

'You've …. you've killed my Trevor,' sobbed Donzo.

Steve couldn't help but grin.

'So it's *my* Trevor is it? So that's what all that anti-gay
shite was about… a big fuckin' smokescreen. Fuck, I shoul-
da guessed. It's always the one's that slabber on about how
much they hate fruits that are the biggest fruits of all. And all
that ballix about what a ride Jeanie is and what you'd like to
do to her… aye, right enough.'

If it hadn't been for the fact that this was one of the mon-
sters who'd taken Doug's life away, Steve might even have
started feeling a sense of pity that a community's narrow-
minded attitudes had forced Donzo into living a lie. But he
kept remembering his dead friend. Doug, the dutiful son who
was forever round his elderly folks' place doing DIY jobs for
them at weekends. Doug, the soft touch who'd always get all
the rounds in when his drinking buddies were skint. Doug
whose eyes would fill up if they were listening to Marvin
Gaye's *What's Going On* album after a night at the pub.

'You dirty murderin' low-life cunt.'

Steve had only seen flying Kung Fu kicks in *Enter the
Dragon* but Bruce Lee had left him with a vivid impression
of the basic technique. Making a crazed monkey noise as he

took a running jump, he made his assent and landed feet first onto Donzo's protruding gut. As Donzo tumbled backwards, the shock on his fat face made him look even more gormless than usual. He teetered for a few seconds, flapping his arms and snorting like a pig as he tried to regain his balance. Gravity got the better of him.

With his work done, Steve got back onto his feet and took a look over the precipice. On the white rocks below, he could make out two blobs of blue and beige splattered with red. Seagulls were already taking an interest. 'Hope they don't mind a bit of gristle,' thought Steve.

28

Steve wandered back towards the coast road with a strange sense of calm. He could see the headlines in The Belfast Telegraph. 'Gay shame leads to paramilitary suicide pact'. Trevor and Donzo's UDA cohorts were bound to have known about their secret love and would now be free to blab about it to anyone who would listen. Their trip to Brighton could be explained by the fact that it was a 'well-known gay resort.' The Northern Irish media would have a field day with salacious stuff like this. He felt safe now and also knew that the residents of North Belfast would be a little less endangered too though he couldn't really kid himself that there weren't a fair few wannabe Trevor McCanns and Donzos ready to follow in their psychopathic footsteps.

From the top deck of the 12A bus heading west, Steve admired the Sussex coast as the sun went down and he could see the lights of the Palace Pier in the distance. Teenagers in the seats in front of him chattered excitedly in anticipation of a night out in Brighton. When the bus stopped at Rottingdean, Steve could hear each of the departing passengers thank the bus driver. A few hours previously, he'd been frantically planning to leave this place. Now he wasn't so sure that he needed or wanted to.

When Steve returned to Lansdowne Place, the holdall that he'd been carrying when he'd been abducted by Trevor and Donzo was still lying on the front steps. He checked its contents and nothing seemed to be missing. Back in the flat, he grabbed a couple of beers from the fridge, put on a vinyl copy of Paul Weller's first solo album and lay down on the sofa.

'Aye, they said oul' Paul was a washed-up has-been when he made this record and it's probably the best thing he's ever done,' thought Steve. He held the album sleeve up and made a toast to it. 'Here's to great fuckin' comebacks, eh Paul?'

29

Steve slept in later than usual and was awoken at around midday on Saturday by the sound of Bobby returning to the flat. He decided it was best not to burden Bobby with knowledge of recent events when he was asked what sort of night he'd had.

'Ach just a quiet one, mate. Watched some oul' ballix on the telly and had a few beers. Yerself?'

'Went out for a couple of drinks with Helen at the Heart and Hand' replied Bobby.

'A nice young fair-haired lady was asking after you, as it goes ...'

Steve felt a tingle of pleasure at this snippet of news.

'Ye mean Sal? Thought she was back with yer man Rich.'

'You mean Rich by name, tight as a gnat's chuff by nature? Nah, she's blown him out for perving after teenagers. Reckon you're in there boss if you don't majorly fuck it up. She mentioned that she'll be at the Sidewinder on Sunday night 'cos some mate of hers is DJ-ing... pretty bloody obvious that she wanted me to be passing on that bit of information to a certain Belfast boy.'

Steve smiled and clapped his hands.

'Right mate, we're goin' for a few wee swallees at the Sidewinder tomorrow night, whaddayasay?'

'Alright boss, anything to help you to get your leg over.'

The easy-going camaraderie that Steve had enjoyed with Bobby since he'd arrived in Brighton had helped him get through his darkest days and as they loafed around the flat exchanging banter, the world of promise and possibilities was starting to reveal itself to him again.

As Bobby pottered about the kitchen making a pot of tea, Steve began thinking about his future. He could sell his place in Belfast and try to buy somewhere in Brighton. He didn't have to work on building sites forever either. Maybe he could make up for his previous academic underachievement by going to college. He'd always secretly fancied doing something creative like photography or graphic design but he'd never discussed his ambitions with his workmates in Belfast because he was already getting enough ribbing just for being a Mod.

When Bobby brought the tea in, he also handed Steve a letter.

'Here ya go boss… this was in the hall when I came back this morning'.

Steve ripped the envelope open.

Dear Steve, It's really important that I see you. There's something I need to talk to you about. Please meet me at the end of the undercliff path past Saltdean at 7 on Sunday morning. Don't worry, Anthony knows nothing about this. Love, Jeanie.

Steve silently passed the note to Bobby.

'Jesus fucking Christ. That bitch is really messing with your head. You're gonna ignore it boss, aren't ya?'

Steve took a sup of tea and made no response but Bobby wasn't going to let it lie.

'I said you're gonna ignore it, aren't ya? Please tell me you're not thinking of going near her again.'

Steve sombrely looked up at Bobby.

'It can only mean one thing mate. I didn't use a rubber that time I had her in the alleyway and you told me that Cubitt never shags without 'em. I'm tellin' ye, I've gone and got her up the fuckin' duff.'

30

The possibility of Jeanie being pregnant made Steve drift help-lessly into daydreams of them raising a child together. Maybe motherhood could be just the thing to tame her wildness, he pondered.

As Steve spent the afternoon moping about the flat in a self-absorbed torpor, Bobby took it upon himself to try to badger him into treating the note with the contempt he thought it deserved.

'So, we've already established that she's a lying, thieving, heartless, coke-sniffing gangster's moll but you're still think-ing you should go along with some cloak-and-dagger bullshit liaison on the undercliff path… get a fuckin' grip.'

'It's not your child she's carrying, Bobby,' Steve snapped back.

Bobby shook his head.

'Look, you don't even know for sure if she's… aw fuck it, do what you like boss. I'm off to Helen's. I'll see you tomorrow.'

Aimlessly channel-surfing on the TV as the afternoon passed into early evening, Steve could hear the chatter and laughter of Saturday night revellers from the street outside. He decided to walk to an off-licence on Western Road to get a few beers. At a window seat in The Bee's Mouth, he spotted Sal's ex, Rich, with his arm around a wide-eyed, willowy-looking indie girl who looked barely out of sixth form. 'Fuckin' kiddie fiddler,' Steve muttered under his breath as he passed by.

Back at the flat, he whiled away the rest of the evening supping his beers and watching an old VHS copy of *Quadrophenia* that he'd found amongst Bobby's collection. Seeing the main protagonist's desperate, solitary search for redemption in an out-of-season Brighton, Steve got to thinking: 'What would Jimmy do if he was in my shoes?'

'Probably somethin' really fuckin' stupid,' he concluded.

31

Steve had set his alarm for 5 am. He'd sussed that there was no buses running at that time so he gave himself half an hour to get ready and an hour and a half to walk to Saltdean. He tried on his blue Levi's sta-prest trousers and brown Hush Puppies with a Brutus short-sleeve gingham shirt. 'Nah, looks far too casual goin'-out-on-a-Saturday-night sorta style' he decided. He changed the shirt for a black polo-neck pullover with a Fred Perry insignia. 'Fatherhood's a serious business,' Steve thought as he fussed with his hair. 'Gotta look the part.'

Steve strolled along the seafront promenade and as he reached the Peace Statue on the Hove/Brighton border, a giggling bunch of students passing a spliff amongst themselves treated him to a chorus of 'we are the Mods'. He smiled and gave them a wave, thinking about the different type of reaction a solitary Mod might get in North Belfast at 5.30 in the morning.

At the end of Madeira Drive, a few lonely-looking gay guys were cruising for company and although Steve got the impression that his tight pants were getting some admiring glances, he wasn't approached.

Once he got onto the undercliff path, he was relieved that there wasn't another soul in sight. This sort of solitary walk didn't feel like the crushing loneliness he'd felt the night before. There was something about walking alone by the sea that reminded Steve of Marcello, a moody character in an old black and white movie *La Dolce Vita* which he'd watched round at Johnny Bell's one night, stoned off his head. He couldn't recall much about the plot but he remembered loving Marcello's Italian suits.

'Stay cool,' Steve said to himself. 'Ye can't let her know that yer heart will be fit to burst when ye see that face of hers …'

Just past a shuttered-up beach café near Rottingdean, an old bearded geezer in baggy faded jeans and a chunky green pullover was casting his fishing line into the sea.

'Excuse me, mate' said Steve. 'Is it much further to Saltdean from here?'

The old boy scratched his beard.

'Would take the likes of me the best part of an hour but a young fellow like you should manage it in thirty minutes I'd reckon.'

'Thanks' Steve replied, 'and hope ye manage to haul in a few mackerel!'

The old boy smiled, gave him a thumbs up and got back to the task at hand. Checking his watch and seeing that it was nearly six thirty, Steve's pace quickened.

He reached the end of the undercliff path with minutes to spare and turned round to take in the view of the coastline stretching back towards Brighton but there was no sign of Jeanie. Looking to his left, he saw the tide was out and smell of seaweed and the sight of rock-pools made his mind drift back to summer holidays with his parents on the Antrim Coast in the 1980s.

He lent against the cliff-face wistfully daydreaming about his lost childhood and soon made out a figure in the distance. He knew it was her. She'd even had her hair cut back into the style he remembered from the summer she'd broken his heart. She'd shown the hairdresser a photo of Sandie Shaw in 1966 to get it just right. He'd always called it her 'killer bob'.

Steve started walking towards her and when she was close by, he saw that she was wearing the original 60s Levis blue corduroy jacket that he'd bought for her from the retro shop in Belfast where Wee Davy worked. It still had the Northern Soul 'Keep the Faith' button badge that he'd pinned onto the breast pocket before he'd given it to her. Underneath the jacket, she wore a red Coca-Cola t-shirt that he also remembered well. He'd complimented her on it as a way of chatting her up on the first night he'd got off with her at The Garrick.

'Hi darlin'.'

A light breeze blew a stray lock of hair across her left cheek and Steve remembered a time when he would have reached over to brush it away. All he could do now was gaze as she talked.

'I guess I owe you an explanation, Steve… but I think I owe you an apology first. You must know that I didn't mean a word of what I said when we had that awful argument. I never had to fake it with you darlin'. You were always amazing.'

While Steve hesitated, wondering if he should just ask her straight up if she was pregnant, she produced a bottle of Pepsi from the inside pocket of her cord jacket and brought it to her lips.

'I guess you must be parched after that walk. Wanna sip?'

Steve took a couple of large swigs and handed the bottle back to her.

'Look Jeanie, I reckon I know why you asked me down here. We didn't use anything that time in the alleyway and…'

Jeanie laughed gently.

'Oh God no, Steve. You must know that I can't bear the thought of rearing some squealing brat. I'm much too careful to ever let that happen. What I wanted to tell you is that I'm sick of this town and I'm sick of Anthony and his gangster friends. It's getting far too heavy for me.'

'So what are you sayin', Jeanie?'

She moved closer to Steve and clasped his left hand.

'Please don't think I'm being crazy but I want us to get the hell out of here and go to Amsterdam together. Remember how we talked about going there on holiday when all the Belfast crew had been saying how cool it was?'

Steve had some vague recollection of a few Mods at The Garrick who'd been in Amsterdam for a 60s weekender and raved about the place, especially the city's liberal drugs policy.

'Yeah, I know it's meant to be a great spot n' all but…'

'But what, Steve?'

'It's just hard for me to accept the idea that you seriously want us to be together in the first place.'

She reached for his other hand and drew herself close to him, her crotch right against his.

'Maybe it's just taken this girl a while to see the light, darlin'. You're such a good guy and I know how you feel about me. You're pure gold and I can't just throw that away for the likes of Anthony.'

Steve could feel his cock stiffen but at the same time he was getting a drowsy sensation that he couldn't put down to the exertion of the walk or the headiness of being in Jeanie's company.

Then he heard a sound that he immediately recognised. Steve's pristine white 200cc Lambretta had been his pride and joy and he'd kept it in perfect nick. The sound the engine made at full throttle was as evocative to his ears as his favourite Small Faces records.

A scooter was speeding along the undercliff path at full pelt, hugging the cliff's edge as it came towards Steve and Jeanie.

'What the fuck!'

Steve could see that the machine was chrome-coloured and festooned with dozens of mirrors of various sizes at the front. The rider, in a sky blue parka, was unmistakeable.

'Cubitt!'

He turned to Jeanie who was now smirking at him and gripping his hands even tighter.

'Sorry darlin' but when he heard about us being spotted together I had no choice but to tell him that I was being blackmailed by some lowlife no-mark from Belfast. Y'know… someone who could drop me in the shit with Trevor McCann.'

Steve managed to wrestle his hands out of her grasp and tried to move out of the way of the scooter's trajectory but he was starting to see double and his legs were feeling like jelly.

'You fuggin' bitch' he slurred, '… there was somethin' in that drink wasn't there?'

'Handy stuff, that Rohypnol,' cackled Jeanie. 'It's not just for those date rape sickos y' know'.

Steve lurched along the path and it felt like walking on a trampoline. Then, just as Cubitt was within twenty yards of mowing him down, Steve saw a huge chunk of white rock tumbling through the air.

Jeanie screamed.

'Anthony! Look out!'

Cubitt swerved sharply to his right but the rock caught him full pelt on his back. He tried to keep control of his machine but couldn't. His steering wobbled wildly and the scooter smacked straight into the cliff-face at the end of the undercliff path. The sickening crunch of Cubitt's helmet-less skull could be heard amidst the sound of chrome crashing against rock.

Cubitt's body lay sprawled on top of the wreckage of the blood-splattered scooter, as if he was trying to give it a farewell hug. On the back of his parka, he'd forsaken the Mod's traditional red, white and blue RAF target and had gone for a more individualistic version in purple and white. Dead cool.

To the sound of Jeanie's anguished, animalistic howls echoing off the cliffs, Steve kept slowly dragging his concrete shoes along the path. After what seemed like hours, he'd only walked half a mile and got as far as the White Cliffs café at Saltdean. There was someone there waiting to greet him.

'You okay, boss?'

'Jesus, Bobby' Steve gasped. 'What the fuck are you doin' here?'

'Did you really think I wouldn't watch out for you? The whole thing stunk to high heaven so I thought it was best if I headed over here to see what shit was going down… I had a great view lying down on the grass on top of that cliff where no fucker could see me.'

'So you saw what happened to Cubitt?'

Bobby shook his head in mock gravitas.

'Yes, it's a terrible tragedy, boss. But falling rocks… it happens all the time. There are warning signs the whole way along the undercliff. Shouldn't have been down there on his scooter anyway. It's strictly prohibited.'

Despite the Rohypnol, Steve hadn't been rendered completely stupid.

'Yer fuckin' with me mate, it was you who threw the rock, wasn't it?'

'Don't know what you're talking about boss. You can't be seriously suggesting that I'd do anything to bring harm to the great man himself, the Ace Face?'

Steve gave him a dopey big smile.

'Ace Face is right. Ye have to admit he looked sharp as fuck, didn't he? Almost seems criminal that such a top Mod died such an undignified death.'

Bobby smiled back at him.

'Serves the silly cunt right for having a target on his back.'

32

Bobby called a cab to pick the pair up from Saltdean and once they'd got back to the flat, Steve went straight back to bed to sleep off the Rohypnol. It was six in the evening before he finally surfaced.

'Alright, sleeping beauty?'

When Steve walked into the living room wiping the sleep from his eyes, Bobby was watching the copy of *Quadrophenia* that had been left in the VHS player overnight. The Mods were in a Brighton nightclub, pilled up to their eyeballs and dancing to Booker T and the MGs. 'Really gets me in the mood for going out, this does. You remember the plan, boss?'

'Fuckin' right! Still game for the Sidewinder?'

Bobby nodded.

'I've stuck a couple of big fuck-off pepperoni pizzas in the oven and once we've lined the old tum-tums, reckon the boys should treat themselves to a few sherbets, yeah?'

Scoffing down fat slices of pizza while swigging on cold cans of Budweiser, Steve and Bobby sat glued to the rest of the movie.

When it got to the closing titles, they tunelessly joined in with Roger Daltrey, belting out the chorus of *Love Reign*

O'er Me. The occupants of the flat below started thumping their ceiling, imploring them to shut up.

'Taxi?' said Bobby.

'Aye,' said Steve. 'Men of our means owe it to themselves, eh?'

'Too true, boss.'

When the cab arrived, the driver was the same ageing rocker who'd driven them to the Hanbury Ballroom a month or so before.

'Alright lads? Lovely night ain't it? Just heard on Southern Counties about Cubitt's accident down the undercliff. What a shame, eh? I tell you what. After I've finished this shift, I'm gonna go out with my brother and get fuckin' rat-arsed.'

When he pulled up at the Sidewinder, Steve shoved the driver a tenner for the five-quid fare.

'Keep the change mate and have a great night with yer bro later, alright?'

Steve had never been in the pub before but he reckoned it looked alright. The bar staff served them promptly, the red-brick rustic décor wasn't offending his eyes and the lights were nice and low. Bobby was taking care of the drinks. A pint of Harveys for him, Guinness for Steve. Just along from the bar area, there was a DJ stood behind some decks. He had his headphones on and was intently lining up a new track to follow on from *The Letter* by The Box Tops.

Steve was grinning and swaying along to the tune when he felt a nudge.

'Hey stranger.'

She was wearing a Small Faces t-shirt which pleased Steve but it was the kindness in her blue eyes that really got him.